THE MUSIC OF LOVE

When Claire Lynton accepts the position of personal assistant to the chairman of MDM Enterprises, she is dismayed to find that he is Marc Deloren, the world famous rock star. Claire, a classical violinist, has no interest in pop music. Also, she remembers Marc Deloren before his rise to fame, and believes him to have been responsible for dropping her brother from his rock band. However, Claire is to discover a side to Marc's nature she never dreamed existed.

Books by Karen West
in the Linford Romance Library:

HAMILTON'S FOLLY

KAREN WEST

THE MUSIC OF LOVE

Complete and Unabridged

LINFORD
Leicester

First published in Great Britain in 1990 by
Robert Hale Limited
London

First Linford Edition
published 1998
by arrangement with
Robert Hale Limited
London

British Library CIP Data

West, Karen
   The music of love.—Large print ed.—
Linford romance library
1. Love stories
2. Large type books
I. Title
823.9'14 [F]

ISBN 0–7089–5261–5

Published by
F. A. Thorpe (Publishing) Ltd.
Anstey, Leicestershire
Set by Words & Graphics Ltd.
Anstey, Leicestershire
Printed and bound in Great Britain by
T. J. International Ltd., Padstow, Cornwall

This book is printed on acid-free paper

1

"**W**HEN I accepted the job, I had no idea that I would be working for Marc Deloren." Claire Lynton angrily faced the wiry little man with the frizzy hair who had interviewed her a week ago. "You gave me to understand that I was to be personal assistant to the Chairman of MDM Enterprises."

"And that's just what you are, love, MDM stands for Marc Deloren and Mirage. You sound as if you wouldn't have accepted the post if you'd known." He stared at her incredulously.

"You're right, I wouldn't."

"Well, you're a rare one and no mistake, love. Most girls would give their eye teeth for an hour in his company let alone the chance of working for him. Besides, I thought you were desperate for a job."

1

"I am." Claire glanced around the walls of the spacious top floor office that overlooked the Thames at Kingston in Surrey. They were crowded with large signed photographs of the famous singer and his rock band, Mirage. "But I'm sorry, Mr Feekes, I really don't think I would fit in here."

When Claire had applied for the job, she had been interviewed in an office in the West End which had given no clues as to the identity of her prospective employer.

Jasper Feekes, who had been Marc Deloren's manager for many years, narrowed his eyes and gazed shrewdly at Claire through a curtain of cigarette smoke. "It's a pity you feel like that love, because I think you would be ideal. The advert had to be vague otherwise we'd get all sorts of riff raff applying. You seem to fit the bill in every way. Your references are good, you seem level headed and calm and you said you were a music lover."

"I am, but not this sort of music! I

play in an orchestra!"

Jasper sighed. "We really have been at cross purposes haven't we? Still never mind, what say you give it a try? I'm pretty desperate at the moment, as you can see." He waved an arm around the untidy cluttered office. "Our last girl left rather suddenly and I'm stuck with trying to arrange a charity concert and next month's American tour." His voice took on a pleading note, "How about a month's trial?"

"Well . . . " Claire sounded doubtful then she remembered how much she needed a job. She'd recently been made redundant and the way things were going, if she didn't earn some money soon she would have to give up her flat and move back with her mother. The thought of that prospect decided her. Squaring her shoulders in her tailored grey suit she looked down at Jasper Feekes. "All right Mr Feekes, I'll try it for a month."

"That's fine, and the name's Jasper by the way. That'll be your desk, over there by the window, love. There's a pile of fan mail waiting to be answered, so you can get cracking on that, O.K.? Marc will be in later so you'll be able to meet him."

Claire moved across to the desk, sat down and for several moments she gazed miserably at the typewriter. What she hadn't told Jasper was that she had in fact already met Marc Deloren, except that in those days, he'd been plain Paul Harris, a sixth former at the same school where Claire had been a junior. She had had good reason to dislike him, even then, hating his conceited manner when he had formed his first pop group and subsequently found half the girls in the school chasing after him.

As she began to open his fan mail she wondered if he would recognise her. She shuddered at the prospect for on several occasions he had come to her house with her older brother, Chris; she'd been plump in those days with a brace on her teeth. A quick glance at her reflection in the black glazed wall above the desk reassured her that her appearance had changed drastically since then. Now, her figure was slender, her dark hair, once caught back into tight bunches was cut short and beautifully styled while the tiny straight row of white teeth, more than compensated the hateful years with the brace.

Over the years, during his fantastic rise to fame, she hadn't altered her opinion of him, in fact if it were possible, she detested all that he stood for even more now than she had in the past. There was no denying his success, his name was now a household word and press stories of his triumphs were as plentiful as his conquests of a whole string of beautiful women, but in Claire's eyes that only made him appear even more contemptible.

Claire worked steadily for a couple of hours moving on to try to bring some order to the chaotic state of the office after she had dealt with the mail. During this time Jasper Feekes was continuously on the telephone, getting more and more wound-up as he made arrangements for the band. Just when Claire imagined he must be on the point of a coronary, the outer door of the office was suddenly flung open making them both jump and Marc Deloren strode into the room.

"Jasper, Steve says the new video isn't ready yet. What the hell's going on?" Dressed in a loose cotton jacket and trousers and an emerald green open-necked shirt, he crossed the office and ignoring Claire, stood before Jasper's desk, his hands on his hips in a gesture of exasperation.

"For God's sake, Marc, do I have to wet-nurse everyone around here? I haven't shifted from this room since eight o'clock this morning."

Claire felt sorry for Jasper and was on the point of backing up his statement by confirming how busy he had been, when Marc Deloren suddenly turned round and stared at her.

"Who's this?" His tone was curt.

"Claire Lynton, your new assistant."

He turned to look at her again and for a moment she thought he might have recognised her although the name Lynton wouldn't have meant anything to him as her mother had married twice and her brother's name was Roberts; then she realised that it wasn't recognition in his eyes but amazement as he took in her appearance.

"Well let's hope you can stand the pace longer than the last one," he snapped.

He had changed considerably since Claire had last seen him, he'd only been eighteen then; now, she reflected he must be thirty for he was six years older than herself. In those far-off school days he'd worn his dark hair long, now it was cut fashionably short.

"Claire is only staying on a month's trial," sighed Jasper, running his fingers distractedly through his blond-permed hair.

"Having second thoughts already, are we?" Marc Deloren's expression was clearly mocking as he took in her business suit, sensible shoes and neat hairstyle.

"I accepted the position under false pretences, Mr Deloren," Claire kept her tone as cold as she could, "I had no idea I would be working for a rock band."

"Not quite your scene, eh?" He suppressed a smile, and his gaze flickered over her again, "Well, no-one's forcing you to stay, I daresay there are plenty who would jump at the job."

Claire stiffened angrily but Jasper jumped to his feet and intervened. "Shut up Marc, don't antagonise the lady. She's got damn good references. She's only been here a couple of hours and she's straightened up this pig sty already. I need her, even if you don't."

Marc Deloren shrugged and without another glance at Claire, disappeared into an inner office where a few minutes later they could hear him in conversation with someone on the telephone.

"Don't let him get to you, love," Jasper gave an apologetic shrug, "He gets uptight when we have so much on." He suddenly looked anxious, "You will stay, won't you?"

Claire realised that her hands were clenched into two angry fists. She took a deep breath, "I'll stay because I said I would, but the next month won't pass quickly enough for me!"

As Claire joined the queue at the bus stop that evening it started to rain. She turned up the collar of her raincoat and wished she had brought her umbrella. Behind her in the queue, a group of girls from the local Polytechnic chattered and giggled like a bunch of brightly coloured birds.

Claire had been relieved when it was time to go home, it had been a difficult day and she longed for the peace and quiet of her tiny flat.

She glanced up as a black Porsche sports car flashed past the bus stop, its tyres swishing on the wet road. Idly she noticed the car had a red stripe down its side and its windows were blacked out. A few yards further on, it screeched to a halt, the driver's window glided down and Marc Deloren stuck his head out.

"Come on," he shouted, "I'll give you a lift."

Claire glanced round wondering to whom he was talking. The group of girls had stopped their twitterings and were gaping at the Porsche.

"It's him!" shrieked a tall girl with burgundy coloured hair.

"Does he mean us?" squeaked another in disbelief.

"Hurry up," yelled Marc Deloren.

Suddenly, realising he meant her, Claire started to run, only too aware that behind her, the girls too were in pursuit of their idol. As she reached the car, he leaned over and opened the passenger door and she fell inside just as the car pulled away from the kerb to the accompaniment of protesting tyres and howls from the fans.

"That was a close thing," he muttered as Claire struggled to sort herself out and groped for the seat belt.

"That's not a very nice way to talk about your fans, after all if it wasn't for them, you'd hardly be where you are today," snapped Claire as she finally clicked the seat belt and sat back with relief.

He glanced at her incredulously. "You've got no idea what you're talking about. I love my fans but have you any idea what could have happened if they had caught me?"

"They probably only wanted your autograph."

"That's all you know about it," he replied darkly. "I'd have been lucky to escape with the shirt on my back, let alone all my hair and as for you, well, being female they would no doubt have lynched you just for being in my company. Now, where do you live?"

His tone was abrupt.

"At the top of Kingston Hill," she replied shortly.

She fell silent as he leaned forward and flicked on the car's stereo then as the heavy rock sound filled the car he turned his attention to negotiating the rush-hour traffic.

While he was occupied Claire stole a sideways glance at his set profile; the high-bridged straight nose and the firm square jawline.

As if he sensed her scrutiny he flashed her a glance. His eyes were a startling blue, an unusual but devastating combination with his black hair.

Claire stiffened. The glance was faintly amused as if he were only too used to female attention and hurriedly she averted her eyes. The last thing she wanted was for him to think that she belonged to those ranks of adoring women when for years she had detested him for the callous way he had treated her brother.

Suddenly she realised he had spoken to her but because of the volume of the music she hadn't heard him. She winced and glanced at the stereo.

He raised his eyebrows at the face she pulled. "Don't tell me you don't like this."

She shrugged.

"I told Jasper to get someone who liked music." He sounded exasperated.

"He did. I mean I do, but he didn't say what kind of music, I prefer classical."

The glance he threw her was incredulous then he raised his eyes heavenwards.

By this time they had driven through the town and as they climbed Kingston Hill, Claire pointed to a large house on the corner of a tree-lined avenue. "I live over there."

He pulled up sharply, his tyres sending a spray from a large puddle over the pavement. Ducking his head he looked up at the pleasant three-storey house. "You live with your parents?"

Claire shook her head. "No, I have a flat at the top of the building."

"Well, love, I'm sorry but I can't remember your name," he spread his hands helplessly on the steering wheel.

"Lynton. Claire Lynton."

"Ah yes, Claire. Well, Claire, I don't think this is going to work, do you?"

"What do you mean?" She turned in her seat to look at him, hating the arrogant set of his head.

"You, working for me."

"I agree." Claire's tone was cool. "But I have told Mr Feekes that I will stay for one month."

"What made you agree to that?" He curiously lifted one eyebrow.

"Mr Feekes was obviously in desperate need of someone to take control in the office. I had already accepted the job without realising what it entailed, besides which, I need the money."

He stared at her for a moment. "I still can't see it working. I don't think you'll cope," he added bluntly.

"And what gives you the right to

assume that?" Claire tilted her chin defiantly.

"The girls we've had in the past were all fans of the band, dedicated followers of our music and in the end, most of them couldn't stand the pace."

"That's probably where you made your mistake," Claire observed coolly.

"What mistake?" The arrogant look was back on his face.

"Employing fans. You'll most likely get a much better standard of work from someone who is impartial."

"You mean someone like yourself?" His tone was amused and Claire gritted her teeth for a moment to prevent herself from making an angry retort.

"Yes, Mr Deloren, that's exactly what I mean. But don't get me wrong, it's certainly not the type of job I was looking for. Nevertheless, I would imagine I'll be able to complete my duties in the office without having to put up with too much of that," she nodded towards the stereo. "I will work the one month that I've agreed during which time, I hope I will have found another position and Mr Feekes will have found my replacement."

"One month," he mused, running his finger round the rim of the black leather steering-wheel, "that brings us up to the start of our USA tour." Then quite suddenly, so that she was totally unprepared, he said. "Have we met somewhere before?"

For one moment she thought he had recognised her, remembered her as Chris's kid sister. It would be difficult enough as it was working for one month beside this insufferable man without having to cope with all her anger and resentment from the past so she tried to steer him off the track.

"No, we haven't met," she lied. "Unless of course I just don't remember."

The barb was pointed and he grimaced.

Claire made as if to get out of the car but he spoke again.

"Did Jasper give you any indication

what your work would involve?"

She hesitated, one hand on the door catch. "Nothing really specific. When he interviewed me he gave me to understand that I would be personal assistant to the chairman, and I naturally assumed that would mean the usual office duties and being responsible for organising the chairman's personal appointments."

Marc Deloren allowed a brief grin to cross his face then he was serious again. "Jasper really is the limit. I'm afraid there's a little more to it than that."

"What do you mean?" She was immediately on her guard.

"Well for a start it's not some cushy nine-to-five office number."

"I didn't for one moment imagine it would be. You don't exactly lead a nine-to-five existence, do you, Mr Deloren?"

He sighed as if he found her cool almost hostile manner exasperating.

"Look, it seems as if we are going to

be forced to put up with each other for the next month. I don't think you're suitable for the job and you obviously don't approve of me or my life-style, but if we are to get along without being at each other's throats, then I think there are a few things we should get straight. I suggest you see me at the office tomorrow morning at ten o'clock."

His curt nod was obviously one of dismissal and Claire scrambled from the car, abandoning all attempts at an elegant exit in her haste. She was fuming as she watched him draw away. He hadn't changed at all, unless it was to become even more arrogant and self-opinionated than he had been in the past.

But at least he hadn't recognised her, she thought with a grim smile as she inserted her key in the lock and let herself into her flat.

With a curiously despondent feeling Claire prepared a light meal for herself. She had left home that morning with such high hopes of her new job and now she found herself working for a man she had detested for years.

She carried her tray into her tiny lounge which she had recently redecorated in shades of apricot and blue and kicking off her shoes, settled herself on the sofa with a sigh of relief. As far as she could see the only bright spot on the horizon was the fact that she had a rehearsal that evening for a concert which her orchestra was performing in Brighton in two weeks' time.

As she ate her meal she turned on the television but she found it impossible to concentrate as her thoughts repeatedly returned to the events of the day. She had no idea how she was going to get through the next month. The very thought of it appalled her. After her talk with Jasper Feekes she had hoped that she might be able to spend most of her time in the office well away from the actual activities of the band, but Marc Deloren had just given her to understand that the job entailed a lot more than that. Whatever could he have meant?

Restlessly Claire carried her tray back to the kitchen, half her meal untouched. In spite of herself she was forced to acknowledge Marc Deloren's phenomenal success, and as she washed up, she found herself trying to recall the press reports she'd read about him and the band over the years.

At first he had been the wild boy of Rock, each performance of the band's tours hitting the headlines for one outrageous reason after another. His private life had been worse if anything, with a succession of starlets and models vying for his attention. At one time she recalled, his name had been closely linked with a certain Swedish film star, then a European princess from one of the lesser-known principalities, but he had never married.

As the success of the band had grown, with one chart-topping hit after another, its image had changed, that much, even

Claire, with her limited knowledge of the pop world, knew. Mirage had been one of the first bands responsible for combining classical Rock with popular melodies so extending their appeal to a much wider audience. In spite of this, Claire had never liked their music and this wasn't simply through her prejudice of Marc Deloren. Pop Music had never been her scene. She came from a very musical family, had learnt to play the piano and the violin when she was a little girl and her love of the classics had stayed with her.

As her thoughts turned to her own music she decided to dismiss all thoughts of Marc Deloren for the rest of the evening; time enough to face all that again the next day, but for now, her time was her own to enjoy in her own way.

Hurrying through to her bedroom she pulled off the grey suit she had chosen as being suitable for her first day at her new job and with a grimace, hung it up in her wardrobe. After a moment's deliberation she took down a full, loose skirt in richly coloured prints and teamed it with a crisp white blouse and a wide black patent belt.

Her friend Jane, who also played the violin in the orchestra, had arranged to pick her up and when she was ready, Claire wandered back into the lounge.

The television was still on and Claire was about to switch it off when she heard the announcer say; "And for the third week running, at number one, it's Marc Deloren and Mirage with their current hit, *Rogue Male*."

Claire's finger froze on the button. Only yesterday in the same situation, she would have switched off immediately, but now she seemed incapable of movement and she watched mesmerised as the band appeared on screen.

Marc Deloren in skin tight, black trousers and a purple silk shirt moved panther like across the stage while the other members of the band were barely visible behind a screen of coloured smoke.

Claire watched for several moments both repelled and fascinated then moved again towards the control switch but yet again, she stopped before pressing it, for this time, the camera had zoomed in for a close-up of Marc Deloren.

He had cupped the microphone almost lovingly close to his lips but his eyes, those incredibly blue eyes that had flashed so mockingly at her only hours before, appeared now to be staring into hers. For a moment it was as if the medium of television did not exist, it was as if he were here in the very room.

Claire stood transfixed, incapable of action, then suddenly her doorbell sounded and the spell was broken.

She flicked off the switch, grabbed her violin case and resolutely went to join her friend. It wasn't until she climbed into Jane's Mini that she realised she was trembling.

"Hi! Sorry I'm a bit late," Jane looked flushed but very happy. "I've been on the phone to Chris."

"How is he?" Claire fastened her seat belt and turned to her friend with a smile. Jane had recently become engaged to Claire's brother Chris.

"He's fine, sends his love and guess what? He thinks he's found a flat that we can actually afford."

"Oh Jane, that's great, I'm so pleased." Claire sat back, content to let Jane prattle on about her plans for the future. Her friend seemed to have forgotten the fact that Claire had started her new job that day and for the time being, Claire was content not to remind her. She found she was faintly apprehensive of Jane's reaction and even more so of her brother's.

She enjoyed the rehearsal which took place in a theatre on the far side of the town. She had been playing with the symphony orchestra for several years, taking part in all their amateur productions. It was her life, she loved it and had long cherished the dream of turning professional as her brother had done three years ago when he had joined the London Symphony Orchestra.

As the strains of Brahms' Third Symphony swept over her she felt herself relax and the tensions of her frustrating day dissolved. It wasn't until after the rehearsal and a little gang from the orchestra were relaxing over a drink in one of the riverside pubs that she was reminded again.

It was Jane who jogged her memory. With her glass of lager halfway to her mouth, she stopped then turned to Claire.

"Claire, you started your new job today!" she exclaimed, "Oh I'm so sorry, I'd completely forgotten in all the excitement of Chris phoning and the flat and everything, how dreadful of me! How did you get on?"

The other members of the group, who were sitting around the table or leaning on the bar, turned at Jane's outburst and looked at Claire with interest.

Claire pulled a face, unwilling to discuss the events of the day in front of them all. "It wasn't quite what I expected," she murmured looking down into her glass. "In fact, I doubt whether I shall stay long."

"But why?" Jane wasn't to be put off that easily. "You seemed so keen after the interview. What went wrong? What's your boss like?"

"He's the main problem."

There were one or two nudges and knowing winks from the men at the bar and Claire felt her cheeks redden. "Oh no," she added quickly, "it wasn't anything like that. It was just, well, I don't think we were quite on the same wave-length."

She was saved from elaborating any further, for at that moment another crowd from the orchestra entered the pub and in the ensuing ordering of drinks and bantering as to whose round it was, the subject was forgotten for the time being. But Claire knew that Jane wouldn't let the matter rest there and on the way home her friend once again asked about Claire's new boss.

"Let's just say, that if I'd been made aware at the interview who it was I should be working for, I would never have taken the job," said Claire firmly as Jane brought the car to a halt outside her flat.

"Oh? So who is it then? Anyone I know? Didn't you say it was some Enterprise thing?" Jane looked puzzled.

"Yes, it's MDM Enterprises and I was employed as assistant to the chairman."

"Well? What's so terrible about that? Who is the chairman — Dracula?"

Claire shrugged, the gesture indicating that it might as well be. "What I wasn't told when I went for the interview was that MDM stood for Marc Deloren and Mirage."

Jane gaped at her in astonishment. "Not *the* Marc Deloren?"

"The very same," Claire sighed. "It's no good, Jane, I can't work for him."

"But is he so very awful? After all,

it is a job and you said the pay was fantastic."

"Yes it is. But honestly, Jane, I don't think I could stick it for long. For a start, it seems I'll have to put up with heavy rock music all day and then there's Marc Deloren himself. He's absolutely insufferable. I've always detested the man, ever since that business with Chris all those years ago."

"What did happen there?" Jane frowned. "Chris will never talk about it."

"No I don't suppose he will, he was very upset at the time. He was in their first group. The one Marc Deloren formed when they were still at school. Chris played with them at all the early engagements, then just when they started to get somewhere, after winning a talent contest on the television, he was dropped without any explanation. I can't forgive Marc Deloren for that."

Jane shrugged. "I'm sure Chris has forgotten it now, Claire, it was a very long time ago and besides, he's doing what he wants now with the orchestra."

"He's hardly in the same league as Deloren." Claire sniffed and was silent.

Jane laughed. "I'm glad he isn't! Just think, we'd have to listen to that ghastly music all the time and besides, I'd never see him!"

Claire allowed herself a smile as she stepped out of the car. "You're probably right, but it still doesn't alter my opinion of Marc Deloren. I've agreed to work for him for one month but in the meantime, I shall be looking hard for something else."

Jane drove away with a wave of her hand and Claire turned to enter her flat. It had been a long day and a difficult one and she was glad that it was nearly over. She felt she needed a good night's sleep to recharge her batteries for her morning confrontation with her new boss.

2

THE following morning dawned bright and clear, the wet squally weather of the previous day only a memory as Claire hurried to the bus stop with slightly higher spirits than she'd had the night before. She had finally come to the conclusion that she just had to make the best of a bad job, at least for the next month.

She had hesitated that morning as to what she should wear; her sensible grey suit and white blouse had hardly made an impression on her trendy boss but after she'd toyed with the idea of turning up for work in jeans and a sweat-shirt, she decided once again on the suit. It was the type of attire she had been brought up to regard as suitable for office work and if Marc Deloren didn't like it, then he could lump it.

It was as she stepped into the foyer of the office block that she realised that the whole building belonged to MDM Enterprises. It was obviously a much bigger complex than she had imagined. She walked across to the lift and pressed the button and as she waited for it to descend, she glanced at her surroundings.

Yesterday she had been nervous and very little had registered. The decor was ultra-modern with acres of glass and miles of tubular steel while the foyer seating, although geometric in design, looked comfortable in the softest of white leather. The work of Andy Warhol was in great evidence on the walls while grotesque metal sculptures that reminded Claire of the backyard of some cycle repair shop adorned the thickly carpeted floor space.

She turned as the lift doors glided open and Jasper Feekes stepped out looking ridiculous in a green tartan suit.

"Hi honey!" He looked genuinely

pleased to see her and a little surprised, as if he hadn't really expected her to come back. "Go on up, I'm sure you'll find plenty to do. Afraid I'll be in the basement for the best part of the morning, but I'll see you later."

Claire caught her breath. She wanted to ask him exactly what she was supposed to do; she wanted to tell him about her talk with Marc Deloren and she wanted to ask him what was in the basement, but he was gone, disappearing rapidly down a spiral staircase in the corner of the foyer.

She sighed and went on into the lift where she pressed the button for the fourth floor.

The office where she had worked yesterday was empty but on her desk was a huge pile of mail. No doubt this was what Jasper Feekes had meant when he said she'd find plenty to do. She worked steadily for nearly an hour, sorting and dividing the mail as she had done the previous day, then she glanced at the clock. It was five minutes to ten. Marc Deloren had told her he'd see her in the office at ten o'clock but it looked as if he'd forgotten.

Claire stood up, stretched, crossed to the coffee machine and poured herself a mug, added milk and took a sip. It was surprisingly good coffee. Suddenly the buzzer on Jasper's intercom sounded and Claire jumped.

Gingerly she pressed the switch. "Hello?"

"Would you come in now please?" Mare Deloren's voice was unmistakable.

"In? In where?" Claire suddenly felt bewildered. Where was she supposed to go?

There was a pause, then with a tinge of sarcasm, he said, "My office?"

Claire looked across at the closed door of the inner office. Had he been in there all the time? She straightened her shoulders and taking a deep breath, walked across the softly carpeted floor. A quick glance at the clock showed that it was exactly ten o'clock.

He was seated behind a massive mahogany desk his back to a large picture window with panoramic views. Claire stared at him in amazement. In his striped shirt he looked for all the world just like any other business executive, as far removed from his usual image as possible.

"Come in and take a seat." He must have noticed her look of bewilderment. "You seem surprised to see me."

"I had no idea there was anyone in here," Claire replied trying to pull herself together. "Least of all that it was your office."

He gave a tight smile. "I've been here dictating letters since eight o'clock."

"Really? Somehow I didn't imagine you doing that sort of thing."

He leaned back in his chair and surveyed her thoughtfully through half-closed eyes. "I think you've got a false impression of what goes on here."

His tone was condescending and Claire shrugged. "Maybe I have, Mr Deloren, so perhaps you'd better put me wise on that score."

"Jasper should have done that, if not at the interview then yesterday on your first day, however I know he's got a lot on his mind. MDM, in spite of what you might think to the contrary, is not just a group of pop stars, it's a multi-million-pound organisation requiring a great deal of administration."

"I understand that," said Claire quickly, not wanting him to think her naive. One look around this office with its heavy mahogany furniture, deep-seated chairs in burgundy leather and thick-pile, champagne-coloured carpet more than confirmed what he had just said. She still felt irritated by his attitude however and taking a deep breath, she decided that it would be best to launch straight in. "Yesterday we spoke of my duties and now you tell me you have been dictating letters, surely I should have been here to take those?"

"I dictate straight onto an audio system." He looked faintly amused.

"Well, if you'll let me have the tape I'll get them typed up for you."

"That won't be necessary, we have a typing-pool with the latest word processing system downstairs."

She stared at him in exasperation. "Perhaps you'll be kind enough to explain just what it is you want me to do? Am I here simply to answer the phone, sort your mail and make the coffee? Because if that's the case, Mr Deloren, you can start looking for someone else right now!"

He smiled, his blue eyes flashing, the smile usually guaranteed to charm women the world over, but it cut no ice with Claire and she stared angrily at him.

"First," his tone was infuriatingly smooth, "I suggest you calm down . . . "

"I am calm . . . " she retorted.

"And secondly, we'll clear up one little point. It's all Christian names around here," he glanced at a file in front of him which Claire recognised as her references. "You're Claire, right?

I'm Marc and the wild man out there is Jasper. The others you'll meet later. O.K.?"

She nodded weakly.

"Next, we need to firmly establish your duties. Just so there aren't any misunderstandings later."

He paused and she waited for him to continue, curious in spite of herself what was to be expected of her.

"Basically your job is the same in theory as any other assistant to an executive. You are employed to see that I am in the right place at the right time."

He paused again and the mocking smile was back on his face as he waited for his words to sink in.

"You said in theory . . . ?" Claire sounded guarded.

"Yes, in practice it's a little more difficult than that. I know that all business executives lead busy lives but my life is a little different from most. Take a look at this," he handed her a black, bound leather folder from the top of the desk, "and you'll see what I mean. This is my schedule for the next month."

It was set out like a large diary and as Claire turned the pages she stared in dismay at the apparently impossible itinerary. She didn't however want Marc Deloren to think that she found the prospect of such a tight schedule in any way alarming, so when she finally looked up, the glance that met his was nonchalant.

"So where would you like me to start?" She glanced back at the page headed for that day. "I see you have a recording session this morning followed by lunch with Beverley O'Neal; I trust you won't wish me to be present at that?" Her lips twitched slightly, she couldn't imagine for one moment that her presence would be required at his lunch date with the famous model.

The look he gave in response to her question was cool. "You will certainly need to come to the recording session, if only to meet the other members of the band, but no, you may make your own arrangements for lunch. The remainder of the day will be spent assisting Jasper with bookings and plans for the Charity Concert in a week's time." He must have seen her look of interest for he continued. "It's one of these huge, open air concerts to be held in the grounds of Chillingham Hall, Lord Fitz-Gerald's place in Hampshire. The plans haven't gone right from the start, I think it'll probably give Jasper a nervous breakdown before it's over."

"What charity is it in aid of?"

Claire noticed a shadowed expression cross his features before he answered shortly: "Kidney Research." Then standing up he shuffled some papers on the desk in front of him. "Just in case you don't think that's enough to be going on with, there are still all the last-minute details to be finalised for our American tour."

"You mentioned that yesterday. When is it exactly?"

"We fly out to the States the last week in August; the tour begins at the beginning of September in San Francisco and ends at the start of October in Chicago. You'll find it a tremendous experience . . . Oh, but of course you won't be coming will you? I'd forgotten, you're only here for one month. Which brings me to the point of this meeting." He raised one eyebrow in that maddening sardonic way that Claire had already come to recognise, "Do you think it's going to be within your capabilities to be running my life for the next month?

Claire took a deep breath. How dare he be so patronising! It was quite obvious that he didn't consider her capable of the job but as she sat across the desk and stared at him she resolved to herself that for the next month, she would do it, not only that, but she would do it well and take great delight in proving him wrong! She realised he was still waiting for her answer. Defiantly she tilted her chin. "I don't foresee any problems at all," she said coolly.

He stared at her for a long moment as if he were still summing her up, then he leaned across the desk, took the folder from her and snapped it shut. "Right, that's settled then. Now are there any questions you wish to ask me?"

"Yes. What is in the basement?"

He looked surprised for a moment then he said, "Jasper really did shirk his responsibilities yesterday, didn't he? Come on, I'll show you." Taking a leather jacket from the back of his chair, he flung it over his shoulder and walked across to open the door, standing aside to allow her to go first.

In the lift he remained silent and Claire found herself slightly embarrassed by his close proximity. He smelt of leather and some exotic after-shave that had a deep musky scent.

As the lift came to a halt and the doors opened, Claire realised they had missed the ground floor and gone straight to the basement.

Huge double doors faced them as they stepped from the lift but Marc Deloren turned and walked down a corridor indicating for Claire to follow him. "Did you know that we record under our own record label?" he asked suddenly as they walked.

"No, I'm afraid not," Claire replied. "As I told you before, I know very little about the pop world."

He stopped before a door and pushed it open, she followed him into a large glass-panelled room, then stopped in amazement at the vast array of equipment that lined the walls. Several men, most of them wearing headphones, worked at the huge control panels while below them, on yet another floor beyond the glass divisions, Claire could see various musicians at work.

A plump man, his face red and his shirt stained with sweat turned as Marc touched his shoulder.

He removed his headphones and taking out a handkerchief mopped his forehead. "We've just called a break, then we'll be needing you. Who's this?" His glance which was almost a leer took in Claire and as Marc explained who she was, she could not help but see the surprise on the man's fleshy features.

"This, as you can see is the control room," explained Marc briefly to Claire. "And this is Joe; he's in charge down here. Through there," he nodded towards another doorway, "is the disc cutting room and over there is the copy room where we make tapes and edit and compile albums. Come down into the barn, as we call it, and meet the rest of the gang."

The other members of Mirage seemed vaguely familiar to Claire from the few times she'd seen them on television or in the newspapers. One of them stared keenly at her and she found herself holding her breath as she realised that he was one of the band's original members who would have known her brother. She still didn't want Marc Deloren to know who she was for she didn't feel she could cope with that as well.

There were five of them besides Marc Deloren and they had names like Spike or Dave which Claire was sure she'd never get right. The drummer, Zac, was the only one she felt she would have no difficulty remembering. He was a huge Nigerian with a smooth shiny head, soulful eyes and glistening white teeth. They all seemed friendly enough but once again, Claire thought she sensed surprise in their reaction to the fact that she was Marc Deloren's new assistant or maybe it was she who was just getting paranoid, she thought grimly, then she immediately dismissed the thought as Jasper suddenly bounded across the floor towards them. He'd removed his tartan jacket but underneath, he wore an even more outrageous cerise-coloured shirt.

"Hi, honey," he said for the second time that morning. "Is Marc showing you around?"

"Yes," Marc's tone was sarcastic.

"Something you should have done yesterday. Claire didn't even know we had our own recording studios down here."

"You didn't?" Jasper looked startled. "I thought everyone knew that."

"Well, I didn't." Claire allowed herself to laugh at his expression.

At that moment there was a series of jumbled commands over the PA system.

"That means me," said Marc. Flinging his jacket onto a chair, he strode across to the group.

"This will go on and on and could get pretty boring," said Jasper to Claire with an exaggerated sigh. "I suggest we go back upstairs, get some coffee then you can give me a hand with this wretched concert. Has Marc told you about it?"

Claire nodded as they walked towards the big double doors. "Yes, he implied you were having problems, I'll be glad to help if I can."

At that moment the mind-blowing

sound of Mirage at full blast shook the basement and although Claire shuddered at the sound, Jasper Feekes, long-conditioned to such phenomena, didn't bat an eyelid.

The rest of Claire's morning was spent working with Jasper on the arrangements for the forthcoming Charity Concert. To her surprise Claire found it all very similar to the functions she helped arrange for the orchestra when they appeared in another town, except of course, this event was to be on a much bigger scale. The whole venture seemed to have been beset by one problem after another and as Jasper came off the phone after yet another abortive attempt to arrange transport, he flung a sheaf of papers in the air in exasperation.

"Jeese, you wouldn't think a simple little thing like one extra lorry could cause so much trouble."

Claire glanced up from the filing cabinet where she had been working. "What's the problem?"

"We need one more pantechnicon for our equipment but all the usual hire firms are fully booked. We have several of our own plus road crews, but we need another for this size of operation."

Claire was silent for a moment then thoughtfully she said: "Maybe I could help . . . " but the rest of her words were lost as Jasper suddenly clapped a hand to his forehead.

"Crikey, love, it's nearly one o'clock! Phone through for Marc's car, then get downstairs and remind him of the time. The lovely Beverley won't like being kept waiting."

"But he knew he was going to lunch," said Claire as she lifted the receiver and dialled the internal number for the private garage at the rear of the building.

"He'll have forgotten. He loses all track of time when he's recording. That's what we're here for, love; we remind each other and then remind him."

When Claire reached the basement she asked Joe if he could remind Marc of the time. From the way Marc looked up at the control room Claire realised that he'd received the message over his headphones. For a fraction of a second her eyes met his, then she saw him look at his watch and frown.

Ten minutes later he had changed into a jade coloured shirt and a loose white jacket and trousers and passed through the office like a whirlwind on the way to his lunch date.

"You'll have to be a bit more on the ball than that," he snapped as he passed Claire, "I should have had that call half an hour ago." He disappeared out of the office slamming the door behind him.

Claire pulled a face and Jasper grinned. "Don't worry about it, honey, you'll soon get used to his ways. He has absolutely no sense of time on the one hand, but on the other, he hates to be late for anything."

"I didn't realise I'd have to remind

him to do everything," said Claire ruefully. "Does it include things like changing his socks?"

"Practically!" Jasper grinned again. "But one thing we'll have to do is get you introduced to Greta Saravolgyi."

"Whoever is she?"

"Marc's housekeeper and if you've got any sense you'll endeavour to get on the right side of her and work closely with her concerning Marc's engagements. Greta detested the last girl we had for some reason and there was no end of trouble."

"Where does Marc live?" Suddenly Claire was curious in spite of herself.

"He has two homes, his town house in Kensington and Whitcombe Manor here in Surrey which he bought about a year ago."

"And where does his housekeeper spend her time?"

"She flits between the two, ruling the roost in both." A distracted look came onto Jasper's face, "Hey, my stomach's crying out for food, come on down to the cafeteria and I'll buy you lunch."

Jasper kept her entertained throughout lunch with an hilarious version of life at MDM and in spite of her earlier prejudice, Claire found herself fascinated by the stories he told. It certainly sounded as if there wouldn't be a dull moment during the month ahead.

After lunch Jasper took her on the much delayed tour of the remainder of the building and once again Claire was surprised at the complexity of the organisation. On the ground floor was a large reception area for press conferences while below in the basement were the recording studios. The first floor was devoted entirely to offices; a typing-pool, a large busy room that seemed to be devoted to the band's fan club and a control room complete with a huge map of the USA.

"This is where all the planning is done for the band's overseas tours," explained Jasper. "You'll be involved quite a bit down here."

The third floor boasted a luxurious boardroom, kitchens, staff rest rooms and the cafeteria, while on the top floor were Marc's office and the one she shared with Jasper, a private suite for Marc's personal use and store rooms which housed the band's instruments and costumes for their concerts.

"However many people do you employ?" asked Claire as they returned to their office.

"About two hundred, including the road crews."

"No wonder Marc said this was a multi-million-pound organisation. I'm beginning to see what he means."

"He has other business interests too, you know. It doesn't end with this, he knows he can't be a Pop Star forever, so he has his eye to the future."

I'll bet he has, thought Claire as she sat down at her desk.

"I'll have to go for a while, love," said Jasper, "Perhaps you could get on with those lists we were doing this morning. I'll be back soon, then I'll have another go at getting that wretched pantechnicon." He disappeared out of the office his usual, harassed expression on his face.

When Claire realised she was going to be alone for a while she turned on the radio and winced at the predicted blast of rock music from Radio One and quickly tuned into Radio Three. A Beethoven Concerto was just beginning and she settled down happily to her work.

She worked steadily for an hour and was so engrossed in her work and the music that when the office door was suddenly flung open, she started violently. Marc strode into the room closely followed by Jasper. It was obvious they were in the middle of a heated argument.

"So, why wasn't it arranged before?" demanded Marc angrily.

"We've never had any problem with either Simpson's or Browns in the past, they've always had plenty of transport." Jasper sighed and ran his fingers distractedly through his frizzy hair making it stick up on end and look wilder than ever.

Marc turned and glared at the radio. "Whatever's that row?" He crossed to the set and abruptly switched it off.

Claire stiffened and had to bite her lip to prevent herself from making an angry retort.

"I don't know who else we can get at such short notice . . . " began Jasper.

"You needn't worry, I've got someone," said Claire.

"It looks like splitting the loads," said Marc, "But I hate doing that . . . What did you say?" He turned to stare at Claire.

"I said, I've got someone. I've hired another pantechnicon."

"You've what?" Marc sounded incredulous.

"Where from, honey?" Jasper's voice had taken on a hopeful note.

"I remembered the firm that the orchestra use when we have a concert in another town. I gave them a a ring and they were free."

"What about crew?" Marc's eyes had narrowed.

"Yes, crew as well," she replied coolly, delighted by his obvious amazement that she had used her initiative.

"Oh well done, honey. Well done! Jasper hugged her enthusiastically. "You're a little gem. What did I tell you, Marc? Didn't I say she was just what we wanted?"

Marc Deloren cleared his throat then gave a grudging nod of approval before disappearing into his own office and shutting the door.

When Claire finally finished work that evening, at eight o'clock, her head was reeling and she was exhausted but in a strange sort of way, she felt exhilarated and quite different from how she'd felt the previous evening.

She came to the conclusion as she crawled into bed that if it wasn't for the fact that it was Marc Deloren she was working for, she could get to like the job. It was fast-paced and a challenge and Claire had always been one to rise to a challenge.

3

THE next few days for Claire followed the same punishing schedules but there the similarity ended for every day at MDM was different. She never knew from one day to the next just what her duties would be, for these varied from accompanying Marc and Jasper to press conferences, to consoling a group of his fans, who had waited in the rain for a glimpse of their idol only to find that he wasn't to leave the building by car at all, but had been whisked away by helicopter from the roof of the MDM building.

Marc's stamina seemed indefatigable and he obviously expected the same standards from his staff. Claire was rarely home before eight o'clock in the evening and nothing had been mentioned about time off.

One morning Marc was strangely

conspicuous by his absence at the MDM building. His diary had merely stated a personal appointment for the entire day so Claire assumed she would be working with Jasper. She had a mountain of paperwork to complete so she settled herself at her desk just a little after nine o'clock.

As the morning progressed however she found herself becoming increasingly restless. It was too quiet. Jasper was downstairs in the basement working out some schedules with Joe and Mel, the band's musical director. The rest of the band had the day off. But it wasn't that; it was something else that was missing and as the morning dragged on, Claire was forced to admit that it was Marc whom she missed.

She missed his dynamic presence around the building, she missed arguing with him and above all, she missed the constant throb of excitement that seemed to bring the whole building alive whenever he was around.

A little after eleven she stood up

and stretched and leaning forward, looked out of the window at the peaceful river scene below. It was a sparkling summer's morning, the early mist had lifted and the heat shimmered above the calm surface of the river where two swans arched their necks and drifted dreamily downstream. A group of children were playing on a raft that was tied to one of the many boats secured along the jetties and as Claire watched, a young couple left one of the boats and began to walk along the towpath, their arms around each other.

Claire sighed and turning from the window, poured herself a coffee. For some reason she felt depressed just when she should be feeling grateful for having a quiet day to catch up on some paperwork without Marc's interference.

Her spirits lifted somewhat when Jasper suddenly bounded into the office. No doubt he would have problems for her to solve if nothing else. She was right; he looked frantic. His hair was standing on end, he had one cigarette between his lips and another behind his ear and he waved a sheaf of papers at her.

"Jeese, I knew it! I just knew it!" he cried. "I knew these would arrive today when Marc isn't here. They're already two days late, they should be signed and put into the post tonight at the latest."

"What are they, Jasper?"

He stared at her for a moment as if she'd asked an utterly stupid question, then he flung the papers onto the desk and slumped down into his chair.

"It's the German contract and if we're not quick with our reply, we'll lose it and someone like Queen or Genesis will get it. Marc really will hit the roof then."

"Well, can't we get hold of Marc? Where is he, for heaven's sake?"

"He's down at Whitcombe Manor, but he said he didn't want to be disturbed."

"Oh, did he? But surely for something like this." Claire sounded exasperated. "After all, it is urgent and he's probably only entertaining one of his fancy models!"

"You're right. Yes, we'd better get these down to him. But I can't go," said Jasper flatly. "I've got a producer from the BBC coming to lunch. I know," he suddenly sounded bright, "you could take them down!"

"Me?" Claire's heart thudded painfully as she fleetingly imagined interrupting Marc and his consequent reaction. "Oh thank you very much. I suppose you've no qualms about sending me down to brave the lion in his den! Anyway I don't even know where Whitcombe Manor is," she added lamely.

"That's no problem," Jasper sounded confident now. "I'll have a car take you down."

Half an hour later Claire found herself in the back of a chauffeur-driven Daimler, the German contract beside her on the seat.

Marc Deloren's country house was in the heart of Surrey and as the big car sped through leafy lanes between hedgerows starred with white campions and grass verges waist high with cow parsley, Claire felt her apprehension growing by the minute. She had no idea what to expect when she arrived and even though her errand could be of vital importance, she very much doubted whether her reception would be a warm one.

The village of Little Whitcombe slumbered gently in the warmth of the July noon and about a mile on the far side, the chauffeur stopped before an entrance barred by massive iron gates and bounded by a high brick wall topped with jagged pieces of glass. He obviously knew the routine, for leaving the engine running, he got out of the car, approached the gates and inserted something into a box that was set into the stonework.

Immediately the gates swung open and as they drove between the fluted stone pillars Claire glanced through the rear window of the car and saw that the gates were closing behind them.

For some reason this intense security only increased her anxiety and she fidgeted nervously with the buttons on the jacket of her navy blue suit. The car sped up a long drive flanked by banks of blue hydrangeas, but at the top, all her tension temporarily vanished as she caught her first glimpse of the house.

It lay in a hollow, its old rose brickwork mellowed by the passage of time, its dozens of tall chimneys of varying designs pointing like fingers to the sky and its hundreds of latticed windows twinkling in the strong sunlight.

Claire caught her breath at the beauty and tranquillity of the scene before her. Never had she imagined Marc Deloren to own anything like this.

Whitcombe Manor was surrounded by stone terraces bounded by balustrades and steps that led to perfectly sculptured lawns and an ornamental rose garden. To one side lay a shimmering lake its surface thick with water lilies and bordered by willows that dipped their leaves in the cool depths.

The drive swept in a wide arc onto the forecourt past emerald lawns where peacocks strutted and preened and filled the air with raucous cries. As the Daimler came to a halt, Claire realised that her surprise was because subconsciously she had been expecting something ostentatious even vulgar, while the house before her was fit for Royalty.

Lost in her thoughts, it was a moment before she realised that the chauffeur had opened the door and was waiting for her to alight. Grabbing the folder that contained the contract, she scrambled from the car, hesitated and looked up at the house.

The huge, oak panelled doors stood open giving a glimpse of a sumptuously furnished hallway and even as she eyed the ornate bell rope, a woman appeared in the doorway.

She was a large lady although her voluminous multi-coloured caftan probably gave an illusion of making her appear bigger than she was. Her untidy hair, which in her youth had most likely been an attractive blonde, was now a nondescript salt and pepper shade and caught up in an untidy knot. Claire judged her to be somewhere in her fifties but it was difficult to be sure.

The woman narrowed her eyes against the bright sunlight. "You are Claire? Yes?" She had a strong mid European accent. "That Jasper, he telephone. He say you come."

"Hello, yes, I'm Claire, and you must be Greta." She held out her hand which was immediately grasped in a paw-like grip.

"Marc is out, but no matter," Greta turned and indicated for Claire to follow her into the manor.

"When do you expect him back?" Claire glanced round anxiously at the chauffeur but decided not to worry any further when she saw that he had settled himself against the bonnet of the Daimler and had lit a cigarette.

"He not be long, he go riding."

"Horse riding?"

"You surprised that Marc should ride the horses? Yes?"

"Frankly, yes I am." Claire followed Greta through the spacious hall elegantly furnished in gold and cream.

"You like cup of tea? Yes? You English always like your tea." Not waiting for Claire to reply she added, "Come through to kitchen, Cook having lie down so we have place to ourselves." The last remark was said with relish as if there was very little love lost between her and the cook.

The kitchen was enormous and with its array of copper pans and range-style Aga retained its old-world charm, but at the same time, Claire noticed it boasted every conceivable modern appliance.

As Greta filled the electric kettle she turned and looked Claire up and down, apparently taking in every detail of her neat appearance. She seemed to like what she saw for she gave an approving little grunt, then plugging in the kettle, she said, "You like working for Marc. Yes."

It was a statement rather than a question and Claire found herself hesitating. There was little short of adoration in the housekeeper's voice when she mentioned Marc's name and Claire was suddenly loath to reveal her own feelings towards her employer.

At last, she simply said, "Marc doesn't think I'll cope with the job."

"And you? What do you think?" Greta's eyes narrowed.

"Nothing so far has been beyond me," said Claire steadily. "But," she hesitated again, "the pop world really isn't my scene."

"There is lot more to Marc than pop music." Greta's tone was suddenly sharp.

"Yes, I'm beginning to realise that." Claire glanced at her surroundings, "This house, it's quite beautiful. I never expected anything like it."

"You are surprised? Yes?" Greta filled the teapot and lifted down a jar of biscuits. "I find this house for Marc; I knew it would be right for him."

Claire silently watched her and wondered how Marc had met her, somehow she seemed more than a housekeeper.

"It was time you came to meet me," Greta poured the tea into attractive pottery cups and handed one to Claire. "We must work together."

Once again Claire felt the older woman's keen scrutiny. "Really? In what way?"

"Well we both look after Marc, yes? You his business life and me here at home. It is good we get together sometimes. Come. Let's sit outside in the sun."

The kitchen door opened directly onto a cobbled yard dotted with tubs of brightly-coloured geraniums and bounded on the far side by a

67

row of garages and a stable block. Several of the stall doors were open at the top and two or three horses thrust their heads out and whickered gently as the two women sat down on a wooden bench beneath the kitchen windows.

"You know about Marc's work for the charity?" Greta took a large gulp of her tea.

"I know about the concert at Chillingham next week."

"Hah! That's nothing!" She snorted derisively. "It just shows how little people know of the good he does. He raises thousands of pounds for the charity and even you don't know about it and you supposed to be his assistant! Huh!"

"Tell me about it," said Claire hurriedly, reluctant to incur this lady's wrath, but at that moment the ringing of a telephone could be heard in the house and Greta set down her cup and disappeared inside.

She didn't return immediately so

Claire leaned her head against the old brickwork and lifting her face to the warmth of the sun, closed her eyes and relaxed. A bee hummed amongst the flowering creeper above Claire's head and disappeared beneath the eaves.

She suddenly felt drowsy and was glad of this brief respite in which to collect her thoughts. Greta had come as something of a shock, as had the manor; it was all in such contrast to what she had come to expect of Marc Deloren and his modern, flamboyant approach to life. This place was peaceful, a retreat of beauty and tranquillity that infinitely appealed to Claire's tastes.

She was jerked from her daydreams by the persistent whinnying of one of the horses in the stalls opposite. Reluctantly she opened her eyes and standing up she stretched and listened. Faintly she could hear Greta, still in conversation on the telephone so she crossed the yard to the stable block.

The horse, a strawberry roan, thrust its head forward, snorting and revealing its teeth as Claire stretched out her hand and patted the smooth fur above its nose.

"Hello there," she whispered. "What a lovely creature you are."

At a sudden noise the horse tossed its head and Claire too lifted her head to listen, quickly realising that what they had both heard was the drumming of hoofbeats and the sound of voices on the still noonday air.

Moments later two horses clattered into the yard trotting briskly over the cobbles, their riders engaged in light hearted conversation. Two Great Dane dogs loped beside them and immediately headed for the water trough.

Claire had the advantage of seeing Marc before he saw her and apart from it briefly registering that his companion was a woman, she noticed nothing else for from the moment her gaze fell upon him, she was unable to tear it away.

He looked so different; the very opposite from what she'd come to expect. But could this be the real Marc, this man mounted on a black thoroughbred, his head bare, his dark hair blown by the breeze, or was this some other image contrived to confuse not only himself but anyone else who saw him?

Dressed in cream riding-breeches, a black shirt and leather riding-boots he appeared moulded to the horse as if man and beast were one.

It wasn't until he'd brought his mount to a halt and was leaning forward to pat its neck that his gaze met Claire's.

She was uncertain of his reaction when he caught sight of her. Could it have been pleasure? Or simply surprise? But whatever the emotion that fleetingly crossed those handsome features, it was immediately replaced by a questioning frown.

"What is it, Claire? What's wrong?" He dismounted and handed the reins to a stable boy who had suddenly appeared, then he walked across the cobbles to where she was still standing with one hand on the roan's neck.

"Jasper sent me," she replied. "The German contract arrived this morning. He said it should be in the post by tonight."

"He's right; it should." His voice was brisk, businesslike, then unexpectedly his tone softened as he glanced at Claire. "You like horses?"

"I love them. I always have, ever since I was a child."

He gave a grim smile. "You mean we actually have something in common?" Not waiting for a reply, he added, "Do you ride?"

She nodded. "Yes, whenever I get the chance." She glanced round and for the first time, became aware of his companion. The woman was still mounted and was staring at Marc, although there was a far-away expression in her large dark eyes. She was wearing formal riding-attire; midnight-blue velvet jacket and hard hat and cream jodhpurs. Her hair which was black and obviously very long was bound up neatly at the nape of her neck in a netted snood. Her deep-olive colouring suggested she was foreign, maybe Spanish or from the Middle East, but the thing that struck Claire most was her undeniable beauty.

For one unreasonable moment, Claire wished she was wearing something different; anything, rather than her staid navy blue suit and white blouse. She was forced to dismiss the thought as she realised that Marc had helped the woman to dismount and had turned to her again.

"Claire, this is Serena. Serena, this is Claire, my assistant."

It was the first time she'd heard him refer to her as his assistant and she suddenly felt ridiculously pleased. But he hadn't said who Serena was. Was she the latest woman in his life?

Further speculation proved impossible, however, for at that moment, Greta appeared in the doorway, waving wildly.

"We'd better go inside and sort these contracts out," said Marc as they all followed Greta back into the house.

"I make more tea. Yes?" Greta beamed at Marc and Serena.

"Thank you, Greta." Marc led the way into the hall, then at a doorway which opened to the left, he paused and stood back for Claire to enter the room. As she passed she heard him murmur something to Serena and glancing back, she saw that the dark-haired beauty was climbing the panelled stairway which swept up to a minstrels' gallery above.

Marc followed her into what was obviously the drawing-room. It was furnished with the same exquisite taste as the rest of the manor with deep, floral-covered sofas and delicate rosewood furniture. An elegantly carved Adam fireplace dominated one end of the room while at the other, in front of the velvet draped french windows, stood an impressive grand piano. The lid was open and as Marc indicated for Claire to sit down, her fingers itched to touch the ivory keys.

The dogs had followed Marc into the room and at a command from him, spread themselves on the rich, jewel-coloured Persian rug in front of the hearth. Marc took the folder that Claire handed to him and taking out the contract carried it to the french windows, where for the next five minutes, he read it in silence.

Left to her own thoughts, Claire once again found herself wondering about the woman Serena who obviously seemed very much at home in Marc Deloren's country retreat. She was amazed that there had been no mention of her at MDM; usually, speculation was rife about the women in his life, if not amongst his employees, then from the ever eager press or his jealous fans. It seemed to Claire that everyone had had a field day over his supposed romance with the model, Beverley O'Neal, but she had never heard so much as a whisper about this one. She imagined she must be another model or possibly a film star with those looks although she certainly hadn't recognised her.

She looked up as she realised that Marc had moved to a small writing desk and was signing the contracts, then she stood up as he beckoned to her.

"Would you witness this please?"

Taking the pen, she added her signature to the sheet of parchment, suddenly acutely aware of his presence as he stood at her elbow. He smelt of the countryside and the horses; an earthy masculine smell, unlike the tang of the expensive French after-shave that he usually wore.

Claire handed back his pen and for a second, her fingers touched his. He didn't immediately move his hand and confused, she looked up at him, only to find an indefinable expression in his dark eyes as he stared down at her.

Neither of them spoke and the silence seemed to stretch for an interminable length of time, but which in actual fact could have only been for a few seconds; seconds that seemed suspended in time.

It was Marc who spoke first, breaking the spell. "What do you think of my home?"

"It's very beautiful . . . " Claire answered, hating herself for losing control of her voice which came out as a husky murmur. She cleared her throat. "Yes, very beautiful, I didn't expect anything like it . . . " She trailed off in confusion.

He gave a short laugh. "Like everyone else, you're surprised at my taste, surprised I have any taste at all. Don't tell me, you imagined something big and vulgar with massive swimming-pools and gallons of gold paint."

She looked uncomfortable and he laughed again. "Go on, admit it; you did expect that didn't you?"

She smiled ruefully. "Well yes, something like that I suppose. All this just doesn't go with your image."

"You mean the image I'm forced to

portray to the public? The image they demand if I'm to remain successful in my chosen field? Did it never occur to you that sometimes I need to escape that image and be myself?"

"You mean you've outgrown the pop world?" Suddenly she was curious.

"Not at all. I've tried to progress over the years, to keep our music up to date and to appeal to a much wider audience but in the end, Claire, it's still a job like any other and just as if I worked nine-to-five in an office, I sometimes feel the need to get away. You've met Greta?" Abruptly he changed the subject. "Did you like her?"

"Very much, I found her down to earth; again, not what I had expected. Is she Polish?"

"No, Hungarian. She came over during the fifty-six uprising. My mother ran a guest house in those days and took her in. Greta stayed and worked for us, then several years later, we were told that my mother had cancer." A shadowed look came into his eyes and he turned away from Claire as if the memory was too painful to share. There was silence for a few moments then slowly he said. "Greta nursed my mother until she died, I am indebted to her; this house is her home."

She wanted to ask him about Serena but somehow the moment didn't seem right and she lacked the courage.

He remained silent for some moments gazing out of the windows at the peacocks on the lawn, his back to Claire. She was uncertain what she should do. It seemed as if he'd almost forgotten her presence and as she now had what she came for, she finally took his silence to mean dismissal.

She cleared her throat again. "I'd best be getting back," she said tentatively.

Without turning, he said, "How did you get here?"

"One of the driver's brought me; Jasper arranged it."

He turned then and nodded. "Yes,

I suppose you had better get that contract back."

For one wild moment she thought she detected reluctance in his voice almost as if he didn't want her to go. But that was ridiculous, he probably couldn't wait to get rid of her so that he could get upstairs to Serena. At the thought of Serena she briskly picked up the contract and put it back into its folder then smoothed down her skirt, suddenly acutely aware that Marc was watching her every move with a look of such intensity that it completely disarmed her.

Turning away from him she made her way towards the door.

"Claire."

With one hand on the handle, she stopped. "Yes?"

"I've been nominated for an award by the BBC. I have to attend a luncheon at Grosvenor House the day after tomorrow. I would like you to come with me."

She froze. Why was he asking her?

Why not that beautiful creature upstairs or one of his other companions?

As if he sensed her thoughts, he explained, "I may need you there to handle the press and the fans. You know, the usual thing."

She relaxed. Of course that was all he wanted. She would attend merely as his assistant. Whatever had made her think he had meant anything else?

"Just one thing, Claire," his tone had changed, was brisk now. "Do you have anything suitable to wear? If not, get Jasper to give you a charge card . . . "

"That won't be necessary," she swung round to face him and found his gaze on her business suit. How dare he assume that she had no clothes suitable for the type of life he led.

On the way back to Kingston in the Daimler she fumed but by the time they approached the MDM building she had had time to cool down and reluctantly, she had to admit that he had of course been quite right. She knew without looking in her limited wardrobe that she had nothing even remotely suitable for luncheon at Grosvenor House.

4

The following evening at around six o'clock when they were carrying out yet another rundown of the USA tour, Claire tentatively mentioned that she would appreciate getting away early.

Marc looked up from his desk, a scornful expression on his face. "Pace getting to you, is it?"

He had not been in a good mood since he arrived back from Whitcombe Manor early that morning and there had been moments during the day when Claire found herself wondering if she had dreamt the events of the previous day.

"No, of course not but I have to go out this evening." Although she felt a surge of anger at his manner, she endeavoured to keep her voice calm.

"A date is it? There's no time for a

love life around here is there, Jasper?"

"No it isn't a date," retorted Claire. "In actual fact it's a rehearsal I have to attend." She flashed Jasper an appealing glance but before he had a chance to intervene on her behalf, Marc had leaned back in his chair and was observing her shrewdly though half closed eyes.

"What kind of rehearsal?"

"I play in an amateur symphony orchestra, we have a concert in Brighton soon."

"Ah yes," Marc twirled a pencil between his fingers. "The orchestra, you mentioned it before. What instrument do you play?"

"Violin." For some reason she suddenly felt embarrassed at discussing her music with him; felt that it would be impossible for him to understand that her music meant as much to her as his did to him.

"Well, you'd better get along then." His tone was brusque. "It wouldn't do to keep a whole symphony orchestra waiting, would it?"

She winced at his tone of voice and with her head down, hurried from the room.

Her own concert was only three days after the big Charity Concert at Chillingham Hall. Claire was becoming very apprehensive that she wouldn't have time for the numerous rehearsals and arrangements that would be involved for both functions.

Later, at her flat she changed hurriedly before carefully hanging in her wardrobe the outfit she had bought in her lunch hour. She had deliberately ignored the chain store where she usually bought her clothes, going instead to one of the trendy little boutiques in the town.

At first she had been undecided what would be suitable then she had seen the perfect outfit. It was a champagne-coloured catsuit in a soft shiny material that clung to her body in a sensual way. Together with the thigh-length jacket in the same material it made her feel decidedly glamorous. It had been outrageously expensive but she had suddenly felt extravagant and knew that nothing else would do.

As usual Jane picked her up from her flat. "Your mother's been trying to ring you," she said before Claire had a chance to settle herself in the car. "She said you're never at home these days." She glanced curiously at Claire as she spoke.

"Do you know what she wants?"

"Yes, she wants us to go for supper after rehearsal tonight."

"Oh no!" Claire sighed. "I wanted to wash my hair tonight and I've a hundred and one other jobs that need doing. Did she say why tonight in particular?"

"Chris is down for the day, and I suppose she thought it would be nice for us all to be together." There was no disguising the pique in Jane's voice.

"I'm sorry, Jane. I didn't know Chris was here, of course I'll come," said Claire.

The rehearsal went badly as these things do when the actual performance is only a short way ahead and Claire's heart sank when the conductor called for extra rehearsals over and above the scheduled ones. She had no idea how she was going to be able to attend with the unpredictable hours she was working at MDM. She was silent on the drive to her mother's, content to let Jane's chatter drift over her head.

As they drew up outside the semi-detached villa in Surbiton, Claire's brother Chris appeared in the doorway to greet them. Jane hurried up the path and kissed her fiance while Claire followed more slowly, then as Jane disappeared inside the house, Chris turned to her and gave his usual, lopsided grin.

"Hi kid, how goes it?"

"Fine," she stretched up and gave him an affectionate peck on the cheek. "And you?"

"Yes, O.K. How did the rehearsal go?" He laughed as Claire pulled a face. "Oh, like that was it?"

He stood back to allow her to enter the house and as she stepped into the hall, he lowered his voice and said, "What's all this Jane's been telling me about your new job?"

"Not now, Chris. I'll tell you later," Claire replied quietly.

"Mum's determined to find out about it," he said in the same quiet voice.

"Yes, I can imagine." Claire pulled another face then forced a smile as her mother appeared in the kitchen doorway at the end of the long narrow hall.

One glance at Mary Lynton was enough to establish the fact that Claire must resemble her father in looks for there was nothing in her mother's appearance to suggest such a close relationship between the two women. There was certainly a similarity between Chris and his mother, for her auburn colouring was evident in her son's thick brown hair and in his beard but there the similarity ended, for while Chris was tall and thick-set, his mother was small and wiry.

"Ah, Claire, there you are; I was beginning to think you'd forgotten where I live." Her mother's voice held a familiar sharpness while her quick, bird-like eyes behind rimless glasses seemed to miss nothing.

"Hello, Mum. Yes, I know I haven't been to see you for some time but I really have been very busy."

"So Jane's been telling me," observed Mary Lynton dryly. "But I would have preferred to hear it from you."

Claire knew from bitter experience that it was useless to argue, so dutifully she followed her mother into the dining-room where a supper of cold meats and salad had been prepared.

Mary Lynton had been married twice, each time to men much older than herself and even today with two grown children and her job as a music

89

teacher she found it difficult to move with the times.

When they had almost finished their meal the conversation moved from Chris's work in the orchestra to his and Jane's plans for their wedding, then as Claire helped herself to more of her mother's ginger cake, Mary Lynton abruptly set her cup down noisily in its saucer.

"Well it doesn't look as if I'm going to get any explanations about this job of yours, unless I ask for them." With her eyes glinting behind her glasses she stared at her daughter.

Defensively Claire glanced around the table. "I had no idea who my boss would be when I took the job," she said.

"I should hope not." Her mother dabbed her mouth with a starched white napkin. "I consider it entirely unsuitable employment for you. The man has a scandalous reputation and as far as I'm concerned, it's a wholly disreputable way of earning a living.

The money these pop stars earn is totally out of proportion to what they do."

"Actually," said Claire quietly, "he does a lot of fund raising for charity."

"That's probably just a cover." Her mother sniffed disdainfully. "The sooner you get out of that business the better."

"Claire's already said she's only staying on a month's trial, haven't you, Claire?" It was Jane who came to her defence.

"Yes, probably," replied Claire slowly.

"I hope you're not being influenced by my past dealings with Harris," Chris said thoughtfully staring into his tea-cup.

"He did treat you shabbily though, Chris." Jane frowned.

"Yes, I know and I would certainly be wary of trusting him again but, having said that, it all happened a long time ago and I wouldn't want that fact alone to influence Claire's decision. After all, he must have had his reasons for sacking me and jobs aren't easy to come by these days . . . "

"For goodness sake, Chris," his mother snapped, "whatever are you saying? Of course Claire will be leaving. There's no question about that. I don't want any daughter of mine having her name linked with such a character as that. I remember him as a boy; a long haired layabout. And quite apart from the way he treated you, there's been all those stories in the press about his wild goings on. Why, I shouldn't be surprised if the whole bunch of them weren't mixed up in drugs or something equally distasteful."

"I don't think you need have any worries on that score," said Claire wearily. "I certainly haven't seen any evidence of drugs at MDM, neither have there been any wild goings-on. But if it sets your mind at rest, then yes, I have only agreed to work on a month's trial."

The matter was dropped then and the forthcoming concert in Brighton became the main topic of conversation around the supper table, but Claire knew her mother wouldn't rest until she had her firm assurance that she would not be working permanently for Marc Deloren. No doubt she too had never forgiven him for the way he had treated Chris, although somehow, Claire couldn't imagine Mary Lynton happily accepting her son as a member of a rock band, even one so successful as Mirage. She had always been fiercely ambitious for her children and was extremely proud of Chris's position in his orchestra.

When the meal was over Jane helped Mrs Lynton to clear the table and Claire sat chatting to her brother. Naturally their talk centred on their music then suddenly Chris said, "Have you heard any mention of Stephan Cole at MDM?"

Claire frowned and shook her head. "I don't think so, who is he?"

"He was another of the original members of Mirage. He was brilliant and he wrote almost all the early material that made them famous." Chris stood up then shrugged, "I just wondered what had happened to him, I suppose he was another one sacked by Deloren after he'd served his purpose."

Later they strolled in the large garden at the rear of the house and as the others chatted about various family matters and her mother meticulously removed the dead flower heads, Claire found her thoughts turning to the luncheon at Grosvenor House the following day. In spite of her nervousness she found she was looking forward to it and could not help but wonder if Marc would win the award for which he had been nominated.

There had been great speculation at MDM, where everyone seemed to think it was a foregone conclusion, but as Jasper had explained to her that morning, these events could be very unpredictable and the most unlikely candidates could walk off with the highest accolade.

"Perhaps Claire would like to go with you." Her mother's voice suddenly penetrated her thoughts and guiltily she started as she realised that she hadn't heard a word they had been saying.

"Would you like to come and see the flat tomorrow, Claire?" Jane's expression was eager as she looked at Claire.

"Tomorrow?" Claire looked blank for a moment. "What time tomorrow?"

"I'm picking Jane up about midday," said Chris. "Is that O.K. for you?"

"Oh no, I'm sorry. I can't." She paused then realised that the others appeared to be waiting for some explanation. "I shall be working . . . "

"Working? But it's Saturday," said Jane.

"Well actually, it's a lunch I have to attend." Claire was uncomfortably aware that her cheeks had reddened.

"What sort of a lunch?" Her mother's tone was both sharp and curious.

Claire took a deep breath. "It's at

Grosvenor House. Marc Deloren has been nominated for an award." In the silence that followed, she was only too aware of the incredulous stares of her family.

"Gosh, that must be some job you have," said Jane at last. "There can't be many assistants who get to attend luncheons at Grosvenor House with world famous pop stars."

Chris remained silent but her mother gave a sniff and the look which she shot Claire was clearly disapproving.

"I'm only going to talk to the press, you know, public relations, that sort of thing," explained Claire hurriedly, but she doubted they understood.

It wasn't until much later as she lay back relaxing in a steaming bath that it occurred to her that she had actually been defending Marc to her family. She had difficulty in analysing why she had done so, for nothing in particular had happened in the last few days to make her change her opinion of him. And in spite of the fact that briefly she had hesitated, she was still determined that she would only stay in his employ for one month . . . but somehow, her family had got completely the wrong idea about him and MDM and she had felt compelled to set the record straight.

★ ★ ★

The following day, Claire took her new outfit with her so that she could change for lunch at the office.

"Are you coming to Grosvenor House, Jasper?" she asked when the manager appeared in the office during the morning.

"No, honey," he answered quickly. "I detest these occasions and I'm sure you'll manage any PR work beautifully."

"Is anyone else going? From here, I mean."

"Some of the band will be there which means of course, the current wives or girl-friends will be in tow."

He grinned and Claire felt a sick wave of apprehension. She felt very uncertain what would be expected of her.

Jasper must have realised how she was feeling. "Don't worry about it, honey. You're every bit as good as any of them. Just go and enjoy yourself. By the way," he hesitated, "did you get something to wear? Marc said you may be needing a charge card."

Claire stiffened, thinking for a moment that she detected a touch of anxiety in Jasper's voice. Most probably they were worried that she was going to show Marc up by wearing one of her suits. "I did get something, but a charge card won't be necessary, thank you."

Jasper stared at her through narrowed eyes and shrugged when he saw her set expression. "Just as you like, but you're quite entitled to charge up that sort of thing. MDM can afford it."

Claire was quite sure that they could and later as she slipped into the champagne-coloured outfit, she smiled ruefully when she recalled that it had cost her nearly a week's wages; money which at the moment she could ill afford. Maybe she should have allowed MDM to foot the bill but somehow, it had seemed to her that if she had, indirectly, Marc would have paid for it and for some reason which she couldn't define, she hadn't wanted that.

When she was ready she walked back into the office and found that in her absence Marc had arrived and was deep in conversation with Jasper. The two men had their backs to her and she paused for a moment in the doorway. It was Jasper who saw her first.

He gave a low whistle of approval causing Marc to turn and face her.

She had applied a little more make-up than she usually wore, highlighting her grey eyes, while soft blusher accentuated her cheekbones. Her hair she had brushed back from her face into a trendy new style and together with a pair of bronze ear-rings and a chunky necklace of the same colour, she knew she looked every bit as good as any of the women whom Marc mixed with.

He was wearing one of his fashionable, light coloured suits and a turquoise shirt. For a moment, as his eyes met hers, she was amused to see that he hadn't apparently recognised her. As realisation dawned, to her satisfaction, his look of surprise changed to one of amazement.

"Wowee . . . " said Jasper, "I think I'll come after all . . . in fact, I'll take your place, Marc . . . you can stay here and meet the video boys."

"You'll be lucky," said Marc. "Besides, you know how you hate these dos. Is the car ready?"

"Yes," replied Claire quietly. "It's all arranged."

As she turned to leave the office, Jasper gave her a broad wink and she suddenly had the rather ridiculous feeling that she had just won a round.

★ ★ ★

Marc was mostly silent on the drive to Grosvenor House but with every passing moment, Claire, sitting beside him in the back of his chauffeur driven car, became more acutely aware of him. He seemed subdued today, the rare mood of animation that Claire had glimpsed so briefly when he had rode into the stable yard at Whitcombe Manor seemed to have disappeared completely. Once again, she found herself wondering if that had been the true Marc and this brash, rather macho image just a front for the benefit of his public.

He fidgeted in his seat, fingering the collar of his shirt. Was it possible that he was nervous? It seemed highly unlikely but Claire decided that even he, with all his confidence, could be under pressure while he waited to see if he had won a coveted award.

"I was talking to Greta on the phone this morning," she said conversationally at last, hoping to ease the tension. "She is going to watch the awards ceremony on the television. She said Serena wanted to see it as well." As she spoke she shot him a sidelong glance to see what effect the mention of Serena's name had, but an almost imperceptible tightening of his jaw was his only reaction.

Claire had found that since her visit to Whitcombe Manor she had been unable to get the beautiful olive-skinned woman from her mind but at the same time, although she very much wanted to know who she was and why she was at the manor, she had been unable to bring herself to ask anyone about her; not even Jasper.

She took a deep breath. "Wouldn't Serena have liked to come today?"

"What?" Marc turned his head, a puzzled expression on his face then he realised what she had said. "Good Lord, no. I wouldn't bring her anywhere like this. Besides, she would hate it, she dislikes publicity." He leaned forward. "We're here. Just look at that crowd!"

But Claire hardly noticed the hundreds of fans who surged against the crash barriers, craning their necks for a glimpse of their idols as one car after another drew up outside Grosvenor House depositing various stars of screen and stage, for she was trying to digest what Marc had just said. If Serena hated publicity then that exploded her theory that she was probably a model or a film star. So why did he deem it right to bring her, Claire, to a function like this and imply that Serena couldn't be exposed to such an event? But then, she thought ruefully as she stepped from the car and he turned to assist her, she was merely his employee while the lovely Serena was quite obviously someone of far greater importance in his life.

Angrily she shook herself and with her head high, almost oblivious to the screams of the girls in the crowd who had by this time almost burst through the barriers and scattered the good-natured policemen on duty, she followed Marc, beneath a barrage of flash lights from the ever-persistent press, up the red carpet, and under the striped awning into Grosvenor House.

Just before they entered the building, he turned and waved to his fans, the charming smile firmly in place now, the blue eyes flashing, no hint of the tension of only moments previously.

Claire found herself marvelling at his capacity to adapt, then there was no further time for speculation as they were shown to one of the large round flower-decked tables in the huge reception rooms.

Two other members of the band were already there; Dave with his wife Jeannie, and Spike who today was escorting a colourful lady who turned out to be a member of a rival rock band. The men stood up and greeted them, then Dave introduced Claire to the other two women.

She was acutely aware that ever since she had stepped from the car she had been the object of intense speculation. Who was she? Who was Marc with today? She had actually heard the whispers as they had passed other tables just as now, she observed the same intense curiosity on the faces of these two women.

"Claire is my new assistant," Mare said briefly as they took their places, but the expressions on their faces as they eyed Claire's outfit quite clearly said that they didn't believe him.

For one moment Claire panicked, wondering if by trying to buy something glamorous to suit the occasion, she had gone over the top. She threw Marc an anxious glance but his expression was inscrutable.

During lunch, between the lobster pate and the veal escallops Claire knew a further moment of unease when Dave leaned across the table and said, "Y'know. Claire, I'm sure I know you from somewhere."

"I'm sure that corny old line won't cut any ice with Claire." Jeannie raised an eyebrow at her husband. "You'll have to do better than that."

"No, seriously." Dave remained thoughtful as the others laughed. "I'm certain I've met Claire before, but it was a long time ago."

"Oh, but I would have been sure to remember if I'd met someone so famous." Claire spoke lightly but her pulses were racing and she was conscious that Marc had stiffened and was frowning, then she remembered that when he had made the same observation, she had given a very different answer, implying that she would not have remembered him. She turned from him trying to cover her confusion and was saved from further embarrassment by the waiter who had appeared with more champagne.

The remainder of the meal passed uneventfully and by the time the television presenter Terry Parkes had taken his place on the raised dais which ran the whole breadth of the room Claire had relaxed and was even beginning to enjoy herself.

A huge video screen had been erected

to one side of the dais and as the guests enjoyed their coffee and liqueurs and the BBC TV cameras moved into position, Claire became aware of a growing tension and excitement rippling amongst the dozens of famous show business personalities seated at the tables. She found herself seeing just how many she could recognise before the award ceremony actually started.

The Princess Royal was to present these much coveted awards and as she appeared and made her way to the dais the whole company rose to its feet. The nominations in each category were read by a different personality then excerpts of the nominees' most recent accomplishments were shown on the video screen followed by the announcement of the winner and the subsequent presentation.

As the proceedings moved to the musical section, Claire glanced surreptitiously at Marc. He appeared cool and unmoved as he waited for his nomination to be read, but she noticed the tell-tale muscle that twitched in the side of his jaw betraying his tension. Glancing at the others she was amused to see that Spike was nervously chain smoking while Dave was sitting on the very edge of his chair gnawing at his nails in his agitation.

The nominations for the Female Singing Personality of the Year had been read, the excerpts shown and the coloured star Georgia Shannon had collected her award and was making her way back to her table. As she passed, Marc stood up and taking her arm, kissed her on the cheek.

"Well done, sweetheart," he murmured.

"Thank you." Her voice was husky with emotion. "Good luck, Marc. It just has to be yours this year." Claire heard the remark and recalled that Jasper had told her that this particular award had eluded Marc on three occasions; twice he had been pipped at the post by Cliff Richard and once by Freddie Mercury.

She found herself holding her breath

as the nominations were read, there were five names altogether; his old rivals included. The videoed snipping of his work was his recent chart topping hit *Rogue Male*, and Claire watched the screen with bated breath, mesmerised by his flawless performance and then joined in the applause with every bit as much enthusiasm as the other members of their table.

Dionne Warwick had read the nominations for Best Male Singing Personality, and as she fumbled with the envelope, Claire's nails bit into the palms of her hands while she held her breath for so long that she felt in danger of exploding.

"Best Male Personality, this year goes to — Marc Deloren!"

There was silence for a split second, then as Marc visibly relaxed and thunderous applause filled the room, Dave and Spike leapt to their feet and as Marc slowly stood up, they thumped him on the back in their tremendous elation.

As he walked to the dais and received his award, Claire felt as if she were about to burst with pride. He took the microphone and thanked the BBC for the award, making it perfectly plain that it had been a team effort and that equal acclaim should go to the other members of Mirage. He walked back to his table amidst congratulations from all sides indicating just how popular the BBC's choice had been.

When he reached the table and took his place between Jeannie and Claire, Jeannie leaned across and kissed him, her eyes full of tears. He turned to Claire and she too, in a purely involuntary gesture, caught up in the general euphoria of the moment, kissed him.

It was only when she drew back and saw the surprised, slightly amused expression in his eyes that she realised just what she had done.

★ ★ ★

The celebrations at Grosvenor House carried on late into the afternoon long after the television cameras had ceased whirring, statements had been given to the press and the award winners had posed for photographs. Much later Claire found herself beside Marc in the car heading back to Kingston. She felt relaxed, decidedly happy and not just a little light-headed after the amount of champagne she had consumed. Marc, she had noticed, had seemed to drink very little but Dave and Spike had been almost paralytic by the time they had left Grosvenor House, both of them giving impromptu performances on the pavement to the delight of the patient gang of fans who were still waiting.

Claire leaned back and closed her eyes. For some reason the melody from *Rogue Male* kept chasing round in her head.

She had been ridiculously pleased when Marc too had stopped to speak to his fans behind the crash barriers and to sign autographs, but she had felt a pang when she had heard some of their comments concerning herself. At that point Marc had signalled to Williams, his chauffeur, who had ushered her firmly into the car to wait.

When Marc had finally taken his place beside her and the big car had drawn smoothly away, she found she had been unable to hide her embarrassment over kissing him.

They travelled in silence for some miles then she threw him a sidelong glance from beneath her lashes. He was staring out of the window, his head turned away from her, the high bridged nose and strong jaw firmly set so it was impossible to guess his thoughts.

She shivered slightly as she recalled the brief pressure from his lips. His kiss had been cool; no doubt he'd been taken aback by her audacity but his brief response had been as spontaneous as hers. Her senses began to swim again and she allowed her eyelids to close and gave up all attempts at wondering what he must think of her.

When they arrived the MDM building was strangely silent.

"I expect they've all heard the news and gone to celebrate but I'll see if Jasper's upstairs," said Marc heading towards the lift. "You see if any of the boys are down in the barn."

The control room was empty and as Claire stared down into the barn, she could see that too was deserted but as she was about to turn away, something below caught her eye and leaving the room, she walked down the steps and across the floor.

Spike's keyboard stood open in the centre of the floor and Clair smiled as she saw it was still plugged in. Bending down she flicked the switch, then after flexing her hands above the keys she played several chords. The sound was curiously metallic to her ears, attuned as she was to the more pure notes from a piano, but she tried them again and as she became more accustomed to the sound, she added more chords, then began to play the melody that had been reverberating in her head all afternoon.

The treatment she gave *Rogue Male* was unusual for she had set the haunting melody not against its usual throbbing rhythm, but to a bolero beat. The combination worked perfectly and she continued, increasing the volume as her inhibitions vanished and she gave herself up completely to the exhilaration of her music.

As she brought the arrangement to its final crescendo and the closing notes echoed round the studio, she leaned over the keyboard, her senses throbbing. It was at that moment that she realised she was no longer alone.

He was standing behind her; so close that she could feel his warm breath on the nape of her neck. She turned sharply and as her eyes met his, immediately she knew that her music had had the same effect on him as it had on her.

Excitement and passion flared in his

electric blue eyes. He took a step towards her, then inevitably she was in his arms. This time his kiss was anything but cool, his mouth possessed hers in a single moment of searing passion that sent her senses spinning into infinity.

5

IT was the sound of a low throaty chuckle that brought Claire to her senses and wrenching herself away from Marc she turned sharply. To her horror she saw Joe standing in the doorway watching them. With a leer that made her shudder he eased himself away from the doorframe and walked towards them.

"I didn't think it'd take you long to get round to that, Marc," he guffawed. "Didn't reckon she was your type at first, but they say it's the quiet ones you have to watch, don't they?" He winked and Claire felt Marc stiffen but before he had chance to comment, Joe ran his fingers across the keyboard, noisily jarring several chords before sauntering back to the door. Then he paused and looking over his shoulder, added, "I'll say one thing for her, she can

116

play . . . that was more than any of the others could . . . " With another suggestive grin he was gone.

Burning with humiliation Claire turned away then started as Marc caught her wrist. "Don't let him bother you," his voice was low.

"He's an obnoxious man." Claire shuddered again.

"He can be difficult, I agree." Marc nodded. "But he's damned good at his job."

Claire shrugged and to cover her confusion leaned forward and switched off the keyboard. When she straightened up, Marc was staring intently at her but with the imprint of that searing kiss still burning on her lips and the undeniable knowledge that her response had been little short of frenzied, she was unable to meet his gaze.

The magic and excitement of the day had dissolved, tarnished by Joe's comments, leaving her feeling that she was no better than one of the groupies who followed the band when they were on tour.

The thought that Marc might be thinking of her in that light finally galvanised her into action and with a muttered excuse she brushed past him and walked quickly from the barn.

He made no attempt to follow her and once outside the building, she indulged in the rare luxury of hailing a taxi to take her home. She felt she could hardly wait at the bus stop in her finery; the beautiful outfit chosen with such care and which now only seemed to act as a mockery of the day's events.

★ ★ ★

The incident in the barn had bothered Claire more than she cared to admit leaving her emotions a jangled mass of confusion and that evening at her rehearsal she was quiet and jumpy.

As they tuned their instruments Jane threw her a curious glance. "Are you

118

feeling all right, Claire?"

Claire merely nodded forcing Jane to probe a little further. "Was lunch at Grosvenor House a little more than you bargained for?"

She jumped giving Jane a startled look. "What do you mean?" She felt her cheeks grow hot.

"Nothing. I was only joking. Hey, Claire, there is something wrong. Come on, what is it?" Jane reached out and touched her friend's arm.

Claire shook her head and was thankfully saved from answering as the conductor tapped his baton in a call for silence.

Later in the pub, however, Jane tried again after steering Claire to a secluded alcove well away from the other members of the orchestra. "So, let's hear all about this lunch, how did it go?"

"It was all right." Claire carefully set her glass down on the table, desperately hoping that Jane wouldn't notice that her hand was shaking.

"He won, didn't he? Marc Deloren, I mean. I saw it on the early evening news. I was at your Mum's."

Claire looked up sharply. "What did she have to say about it?"

"She switched the telly off — she had that buttoned up look on her face . . . you know the one I mean?"

"Only too well." Claire pulled a face then was forced to smile as Jane gave a peal of laughter.

"She really hates your boss, doesn't she?"

Claire nodded. "Yes, but she has a false impression of him. There's a lot more to him than people realise. Oh, I know he's had a reputation in the past," she said hurriedly, seeing Jane's look of surprise. "But his housekeeper was telling me about the thousands he raises for charity that no one ever knows about."

"Okay, you don't have to convince me." Jane laughed then added darkly, "But I think you'll have a bit of trouble convincing your mum."

"Mum's always been an intellectual snob, you know that. Pop music, to her, is the lowest of the low and of course she's prejudiced because of what happened to Chris."

"She does have a point there."

Claire sighed. "Yes, I know."

"Have you asked Marc Deloren why he dropped Chris all those years ago?"

Claire shook her head. "No, and I don't intend to. He still doesn't know who I am and I want it to stay that way." She fell silent, only too aware that she had been defending Marc Deloren to Jane. She knew she mustn't lose sight of the fact that he had treated her brother badly anymore than she could allow him to imagine she was easy prey and could be added to his list of conquests.

She drained her glass and stood up. "Ready to go, Jane? I've a heavy schedule tomorrow."

"But tomorrow's Sunday," Jane protested as she followed Claire from the pub.

"Try telling that to my boss," replied Claire. "At MDM every day's the same."

For the next few days Claire threw herself into preparations for the Charity Concert and when she wasn't involved in that, with her own rehearsals. It was a hectic time but she welcomed it for it helped her to overcome her embarrassment over what had happened after the awards ceremony.

The first time she saw Marc after that fateful day, his attitude appeared to be one of faint amusement and this only served to make her all the more determined not to give him so much as a scrap of encouragement in the future. She had little doubt that he imagined she must have been thrilled by his advances as every other woman in his life had probably been.

What she wasn't prepared to admit, even to herself was that, yes, she had been thrilled. The intensity of her response had both shocked and dismayed her, for while Claire hadn't been short of romantic attachments in the past, none had ever had quite the effect that Marc Deloren had evoked.

Activities at MDM grew more frenzied during the build-up to the concert and on the day Claire was up at dawn and ready and waiting when Jasper arrived in his battered Volvo to take her down to Chillingham Hall in Hampshire. There were many last minute arrangements to be made and Claire knew the responsibility for these lay firmly on hers and Jasper's shoulders.

The morning was grey and overcast and as they headed for the A3, the steady drizzle turned to a more persistent downpour.

"This is all we need," grumbled Jasper as he frantically wiped the windscreen with an old duster. "There's nothing quite like a wet concert to raise everyone's spirits."

"It's got plenty of time to clear up before tonight," said Claire with more optimism than she was feeling.

"Or get worse . . . " Jasper was clearly not in a positive frame of mind so Claire fell silent spending the rest of the journey locked in her own thoughts. She'd had a tough time the previous evening when she'd been forced, through pressure of work, to miss a crucial rehearsal and this morning she was feeling emotionally drained. Her own concert was only a few days ahead and she knew her conductor would rapidly lose patience with her if she let him down much more.

Suddenly she realised Jasper had said something and she'd been so lost in her thoughts, she hadn't heard a word. "I'm sorry Jasper, what did you say?"

He grinned. "I thought you'd gone to sleep. Mind you, I wouldn't blame you, not with the hours we've been keeping lately. All I said was, have you noticed how tense Marc's been for the last few days?"

Claire shrugged. "I had, but I'd simply put it down to pre-concert nerves." She turned to look at Jasper. "Do you think it's more than that?"

"Well, let's put it this way; usually before a show of this calibre, he's elated, you know, on a high. But this time he seems moody and on edge. Yesterday he was like a bear with a sore head. Something's probably gone wrong in his love life. I was glad when he cleared off down to Whitcombe, out of the way."

So that was where he had gone, Claire thought with a pang; down to the peace and solitude of Whitcombe Manor, the administrations of the devoted Greta . . . and of course the dusky charms of the beautiful Serena.

She swallowed and looked out of the window at the tunnel of dripping trees and the clouds of spray from the other vehicles on the wet road ahead. What should it matter to her if he was with Serena? He was nothing to her. So why then did she feel so depressed?

She was in the same frame of mind some time later when they turned into the entrance of Chillingham Hall, the Volvo's tyres scrunching on the wet gravel of the drive as Jasper barely slowed down.

The Hall was a vast sprawling mansion of grey stone majestically designed with balustrades and porticos and set in acres of lush parkland. At any other time Claire would have been entranced by the splendour of the scene before her, but today she only had eyes for the familiar red-and-white helicopter standing on the grass.

"I wish he'd make up his mind." Jasper sighed with exasperation. "He said he was going to keep right out of things until tonight and leave us to get on with it." With a squeal of tyres he brought the car to a halt on the forecourt and two figures beneath a striped awning on the terrace, turned at the sudden sound.

Claire felt her heart thud uncomfortably as through the windscreen, her eyes met Marc's. He looked relaxed and handsome in black Levis, a red roll-neck sweater and a black jacket. Suddenly she felt her spirits lift. As she stepped from the car Jasper hurried round, unfurling his brightly coloured golf umbrella and as the two of them made a dash for the terrace, he muttered, "The guy with Marc is Lord Fitz-Gerald . . . just thought you should know . . . "

"Thanks," Claire murmured. When they reached the terrace, pleasantries and introductions were exchanged then as Lord Fitz-Gerald disappeared inside the house, Marc frowned and looked at his watch.

"You're late." His tone was accusing.

"Traffic was abominable," replied Jasper, unperturbed.

"You should have left earlier."

"Come off it, Marc," Jasper spread his hands. "We were up half the night as it was. And we don't all have superior forms of transport." He nodded towards the helicopter as he spoke, then added, "Mind you, if we'd known you were going to honour us with your company,

127

we would have hitched a lift."

"I didn't decide myself until this morning," replied Marc stiffly. "But now that you are both here, you'd better get to work. Lord Fitz-Gerald has put the large room off the terrace at our disposal so all operations can be directed from there."

He turned away and Jasper looked at Claire and pulled a face. Without a word she followed the two men across the terrace and into Chillingham Hall.

Behind the Hall, beyond a row of centuries-old macrocarpa trees was the ruin of an ancient abbey. Covered in creeping ivy and moss, its few remaining walls were crumbling and unsafe but it provided a perfect backdrop for a concert. Claire and Jasper stood with Marc and watched from the window as an army of construction workers built a platform and erected two huge screens from which even the furthest fans would be able to view their idol. Around the parkland that formed the arena, several marquees stood ready to house bars and refreshments.

"So what are the problems?" asked Jasper gloomily. "There are bound to be umpteen, but let's have them one at a time."

"The weather's the chief worry," Marc replied glancing anxiously at the still overcast sky. "The men are already working under protest and only then with an incentive bonus."

"Well, we can't do much about the weather," said Claire crisply. "So let's start with something we can control."

Marc turned sharply and stared at her and for a moment she thought he was about to make an irritable reply, then he thrust his hands into his trouser pockets and wandered moodily from the room.

"My God, I wish he'd stayed at home." Jasper threw up his hands. "What the hell is wrong with him?"

"I've no idea," replied Claire coolly. "But I'm not going to let him get to me. I've far too much to do. If you'll go and check with the electricians, Jasper, I'll ring the press."

* * *

For the rest of the day Claire worked quietly and efficiently, solving one problem after another. In her classic navy blue suit and crisp white shirt and with her beautifully cut hair dark and shining she was to be found in virtually every corner, from the arena to the Hall, the coach-parks to the refreshment tents. She sorted out a dispute amongst the electricians, calmed the frayed nerves of the caterers, spoke to the press, checked the accommodation for the supporting bands who arrived earlier than expected and generally supervised the smooth running of the entire operation.

Throughout it all, however, she was acutely aware of Marc's presence, his continuing air of pent up tension and his moodiness and on more than one occasion, she caught him watching her.

By lunchtime the sky had thankfully lightened, chinks of blue appeared between the grey and by mid afternoon the sun was shining, drying the puddles on the arena and promising a clear calm night. The pantechnicons had arrived early and the band's vast array of equipment had been unpacked and assembled on stage and as Claire gave a final check, Jasper who was talking to Dave, called her across.

"Have you eaten anything today, honey?" He looked so concerned that Claire laughed.

"No, but I'm working on it. I was just about to take five minutes' break."

"She's like some sort of miracle worker," said Dave with a grin. "I've never known an event so well organised before."

Jasper sighed, running his fingers through his frizzy hair. "I know, God knows how we'll manage without her."

"Why, where's she going?"

"We could only persuade her to take the job for a month," explained Jasper.

"But why?" Dave looked bewildered.

"She says it isn't her scene, don't you, love?" Jasper looked at Claire who suddenly felt self-conscious.

"Well, you could have fooled me." Dave let out a long whistle. "I'd have thought you were born to this sort of thing. Why, Joe says you even play . . ."

"Yes, but classical music," Claire interrupted swiftly then fell silent wondering with a sickening thud what else the obnoxious Joe had chosen to tell them.

"Can't see the difference myself." Dave rubbed the back of his neck. "As far as I'm concerned, music is music, you either love it or you don't."

To cover her confusion Claire muttered an excuse and moved away, only too conscious that the two men watched her as she left the stage.

Helping herself to a coffee and a packet of biscuits from a machine she made her way to the large room off the terrace where they had been directing operations. She was relieved to find it empty and decided to take advantage of the rare moment's respite.

Sinking into a leather armchair she set her coffee down on a small table beside her and kicking off her shoes gave a deep sigh. Resting her head against the high back of the chair she briefly closed her eyes.

She awoke with a start to find Marc sitting watching her from the chair opposite. The coffee beside her had gone cold.

"Oh, I must have dropped off," she mumbled trying to hide her embarrassment and at the same time wondering how long he had been watching her sleep.

"You must have needed it," he remarked. "In fact, you must be exhausted, you haven't stopped all day."

"Well, that's quite enough." She struggled to get out of the deep chair. "There's still work to be done."

He stood up and stopped her with a

gesture. "Stay where you are. I'll get you another coffee."

Something in his tone prevented her from arguing and within minutes he was back with two mugs of fresh coffee and a packet of sandwiches.

"Oh, I really don't think I could," she began, then trailed off as he handed her the packet.

"Just eat," he commanded.

Meekly she peeled off the film wrapping and took a small bite of the sandwich. Surprisingly, it tasted very good and as she ate, she realised that she really was very hungry. She finished the sandwiches in silence and it wasn't until she was sipping her coffee that Marc finally spoke.

"Claire, there's something I want to ask you."

She looked up, startled by something in his tone then as her eyes met the steady blue stare of his, her heart jumped crazily.

"I want you to stay with us for the American Tour."

"Oh, I don't think so . . . " Again she attempted to stand up.

"Will you please sit still for a moment and listen to me."

She sank back into the chair.

"Your organisation of today's events has been superb. Everyone has commented on it."

"It isn't over yet." She gave a weak laugh. "It could all go wrong tonight."

"It won't, I can assure you. Believe me, Claire, I know about these things and when something has been as well arranged as this concert, it goes like clockwork. If anything does go wrong, it'll be my fault or an act of God. No, Claire, I would like you to stay because I don't know how we could go back to managing without you."

With a pang she noticed he had said 'we' and not 'I'. "I expect you'd cope," she said lightly then when he remained silent, she added, "Talking of coping, Jasper has been worried about you. He thinks you've been very tense."

Marc shrugged. "Pre-concert nerves

probably — there'll be a few thousand out there, you know," he added when he saw her doubtful expression.

"That may be so, but Jasper said it isn't like you to be nervous."

"Jasper worries far too much."

She shrugged then as she noticed a far-away look come into his eyes, she said quietly, "If there is something bothering you is there anything I can do to help?"

He hesitated and for a moment she thought he was going to confide something to her. Her heart lurched crazily. What had she done? How could she bear it if he starting talking of his relationship with Serena?

"Yes, Claire," he said, "there is something you can do."

She held her breath.

"I want you to say that you'll at least think about staying with us. Will you do that? Please?"

She stood up and her relief at his reply caused her to answer in a flippant fashion. "I'll think about it." Boldly she looked up at him then added, "On one condition."

His eyes widened then an amused expression came into them as he stretched out his hand and enquiringly tilted her chin.

For a moment her courage deserted her then gently he prompted her.

"Well?"

She swallowed, acutely aware now of his nearness, the manly odour of him combined with the musky scent of his after-shave, and the touch of his firm fingers under her chin. "I have my own concert on Sunday . . . in . . . in Brighton," she faltered. "I should like some time to rehearse, that is, when all this is over," she added hastily as he raised his eyebrows. Then before she had time to think, he leaned forward and softly kissed her forehead.

"You take all the time you want," he murmured. "You've earned it — on condition of course that you come up with the answer I want."

"That isn't fair," she protested.

"What is fair?" he replied as he drew her into his arms.

For a moment Claire forgot her resolve to keep this man at arm's length and as his mouth possessed hers she surrendered willingly to his kiss, a kiss so full of fire and passion that once again its intensity evoked a response that both shocked and amazed her.

Finally it took every ounce of her self-control to pull away from him and handle the situation in a light-hearted manner.

"Really, Mr Deloren, what would your fans think of that?" With a nervous laugh, but well aware that her cheeks were flaming she pushed back her dishevelled hair, then to hide her confusion she stepped towards the window. "Talking of fans, it looks as if they've started to arrive already — look, there are several coaches in the car park and Jasper said some of them have been camping outside the gates for days." She spoke rapidly to hide her embarrassment, "Imagine that . . . why . . . "

"Claire!" He halted her prattle of words and she turned and threw him a startled look. "Claire, I need to talk to you." His tone had softened then with an impatient sigh, he broke off as Jasper suddenly bounded into the room.

"Oh there you are, Marc. The guys from the other groups are in the bar. Are you going to join them for a drink . . . ?" He trailed off sensing the atmosphere in the big room and looked quickly from Marc to Claire then back to Marc. "What is it? What's up?" A note of hysteria crept into his voice and as Marc shrugged and turned away, it was Claire who came to the rescue.

"Relax Jasper, there's nothing wrong. Marc is fine — everything is going according to plan. It's going to be the greatest concert ever. Isn't it, Marc?"

"What?" He looked round sharply then as his eyes met hers, he must have seen her silent plea and it was as if he visibly pulled himself together. Straightening his shoulders he took a deep breath. "Right, Jasper," he said firmly, "Let's go and meet our co-stars. Lead on!"

Jasper still looked suspicious as if he expected Marc to say that the concert was all off, but as Marc passed Claire, he gave her a secret smile and she knew as she watched the two men leave the room that his tension had gone and he was ready to face his public.

Her own feelings however were chaotic for while she could no longer ignore the growing attraction between them she also knew she had to discourage him for it could only lead to heartbreak. As if that weren't enough she was also left wondering what it was he had wanted to talk to her about.

6

CLAIRE had never been to anything remotely like a pop concert before and was unprepared for the euphoric atmosphere as the arena rapidly filled. Jasper had found her a corner to the side of the vast platform which, whilst well away from the fans, afforded her a good view of the stage.

As the shrewd little manager had predicted, the ivy covered walls of the ruined abbey indeed formed a dramatic backdrop for the platform. And to add an even greater sense of magic the vast, star studded sky was perfectly clear and a low moon added its glow to the dozens of arc lights that illuminated the arena. The supporting groups received an enthusiastic response from the audience who were many thousand strong, the sea of their pale faces reminding Claire of rows of ghosts in the strange light.

By the time Marc Deloren and Mirage took to the stage the fans were at fever pitch, the din of their welcome was deafening and Claire wondered how the band would make themselves heard. She needn't have worried; the amplification alone was enough to awaken the dead but miraculously, as Marc began to sing, the vast throng fell silent, simply swaying to show their appreciation. But as the last notes of *Rogue Male* reverberated around the arena and bounced back from the walls of the old abbey, a great roar rose from thousands of throats and Claire felt her spine tingle with emotion.

As one number followed another she had eyes only for Marc. Dressed entirely in black, his boundless energy, his magnetism and his sheer professionalism held her spellbound and she found herself enjoying the very music she had previously so despised. Once she caught Jasper grinning at her from the far side of the platform and triumphantly she gave him a thumbs up sign.

The sky darkened, the moon rose higher and clouds of soft, coloured smoke floated gently from the platform and hung wraithlike above the arena and around the jagged walls of the ruins.

As the band prepared for their finale, Marc made an announcement. He was standing at the front of the stage where he had been bantering with a group of fans in the front row who had been trying all evening to touch him. Then unexpectedly he said, "The next number is for a very special lady," he paused while the fans squealed. "No, I'm not going to tell you her name but she's here tonight and she knows who she is." He swung round to the band, "Right lads, let's take it away."

As the band went into the first few bars of the haunting rhythm of *Stay With Me* which had been one of their early successes, Marc turned and looked across the platform towards

Claire and her heart leapt crazily as she listened to the words; *Stay with me, stay with me; Say you'll never go.*

Surely he couldn't mean her? But then who? Was Serena here or could it be for some other girl in the audience whom she knew nothing about. The words were ironic in view of the fact that he had asked her to stay with the band only hours previously and as the last notes died away to yet another storm of ecstatic applause, he again turned towards her and this time he stretched out his hand, leaving her in no doubt that it had indeed been for her.

The concert continued into the early hours with impromptu performances from Mirage and the supporting groups for those fans who found it impossible to tear themselves away. Then when it was all over, Claire found herself caught up in the vast dismantling operation which she had naively assumed would wait until the following day.

At last, around dawn she was able

to think longingly about the room at the Hall that had been reserved for her and as wearily she made her way across the terrace, Marc suddenly stepped out of the shadows, barring her way.

"Claire." His voice was soft. "You must be exhausted."

"I am, but it's all been worth it — it was such a success."

He smiled in the half light and she could see that he too was suffering from fatigue.

"Jasper's ecstatic — he's just told me that there were ten thousand more fans than we'd hoped for, and they weren't all youngsters either."

"It must be your fatal charm that appeals to the older woman."

He shook his head. "Don't you believe it. It's teamwork that counts and after today, there's no doubt you're a key member of the team." Reaching out he touched her cheek. "Thank you, Claire. Now go and get some rest, you've earned it."

She turned and entered the Hall and

in spite of her tiredness she felt as if she were walking on air. As her head touched the pillow her last waking thought was of Marc and the song he had dedicated to her.

She only slept for a few hours then she rose, ready to get back to work, the thought of seeing Marc banishing all traces of fatigue as she grabbed a hasty breakfast with the other members of the band. It was only then that she learned that Marc had gone. Even before the sun was up, without going to bed, he had left in his helicopter for Whitcombe Manor.

★ ★ ★

Sunday dawned bright and sunny with a fresh breeze that swept fluffy clouds across a summer sky. Claire and her family left Surbiton in her brother's Citroen and headed for Brighton.

Her mother travelled with them as both she and Chris had tickets to watch the two girls perform with their orchestra that afternoon.

No sooner had Claire scrambled into the back of the car beside her mother than she was questioned about the concert.

"Were you there, Claire?" she asked sharply.

"Of course, it's my job, Mum."

"But there was trouble afterwards. It said so on the news. A fight, they said, between some of those dreadful hippie types that were camping outside. Mind you," she went on not giving Claire a chance to explain, "it's just what you'd expect. It didn't surprise me one bit . . . "

"Mum, there was a scuffle, that's all. No one was hurt, the police broke it up immediately."

Jane swivelled round to face them. "The concert raised a hell of a lot for charity — kidney research, wasn't it?"

Mrs Lynton sniffed. "That may be so, but it doesn't alter my opinion of Paul Harris."

Claire sighed and looked out of the

window. She hoped her mother wasn't going to keep on running Marc down. She just didn't feel in the mood to cope with it. She hadn't seen Marc since the concert. He'd disappeared down to Whitcombe and hadn't returned and Claire had found herself constantly tormented by images of him with Serena.

"So when are you leaving?" Her mother's voice persisted in her ear.

"What do you mean?" Claire was starting to feel irritated.

"The job." Her mother gave an exasperated sigh. "You said you weren't staying for long, so when are you leaving?"

"Oh, Mum, I don't know. Please just leave it, will you?"

"There's no need to take that attitude, Claire. It's you I'm concerned about. He's an unsavoury character and I've told you before I don't like you being associated with him . . . "

"I like the sound of today's programme, Claire." Mercifully the

148

sound of Chris's voice from the front seat interrupted his mother's flow of words and Claire breathed a sigh of relief as the conversation was diverted and she and Jane eagerly began to discuss their music.

The concert was a single matinée performance and was to be held in a new conference centre on the seafront. When they arrived they were entertained to lunch then Jane and Claire joined the other members of the orchestra to change and prepare for the performance while Chris and his mother took their seats in the theatre. It was a modern complex with the audience arranged around the stage.

Claire was still feeling irritated with her mother and on edge with herself in spite of the fact that she knew she was looking her best. She had chosen to wear a dress of deep burgundy in crushed velvet which accentuated her slim waist and showed off her creamy complexion and dark shining hair. Jane was in black, a full-skirted dress with ruched sleeves, while her lovely blonde hair she had caught up into an attractive coil. Together with the other women who formed the string section of the orchestra they filed through the audience to their places.

Claire glanced around looking for Chris and her mother and it was then that she saw him. He was sitting alone at the end of a row, an empty seat beside him. It was such a shock to see him there that Claire stiffened and faltered, almost causing Jane to collide with her.

Somehow she managed to reach her seat and desperately tried to concentrate on tuning her violin as her thoughts teemed crazily in her head. What was he doing here? Whatever had possessed him to come to a classical concert? He didn't even like her sort of music. He would be bored to tears. What if he was recognised? He would be mobbed. Then she smiled. The possibility of Marc Deloren being recognised by anyone in this audience, let alone mobbed was ludicrous.

At that moment to a storm of applause, the conductor appeared and took his place. The great centre fell silent and Claire, lifting her bow, tried desperately to concentrate on the opening item, an Hungarian Rhapsody.

Gradually however she relaxed and as one movement followed another, in spite of her acute awareness of Marc's presence, she gave herself up to the exhilaration of her music and played as she never had before.

After the concert, to Claire's relief, there was no sign of Marc. While part of her longed to see him, she dreaded the explanations that would surely follow if he met her family.

The two girls met Mrs Lynton and Chris for afternoon tea in the restaurant before their journey home.

"It was a delightful concert." Mrs Lynton was generous in her praise as she poured the tea.

"Wonderful," agreed Chris. "You

girls played very well."

"Well, Claire certainly did," said Jane with a grin. "She played like someone possessed — I think the conductor wondered what had hit him. He came round afterwards and offered her a solo spot in the next concert."

Claire blushed amid the congratulations of her family and as she sipped her tea, she failed to notice the sudden silence that had fallen on the little group. Then as Chris slowly rose to his feet, she glanced over her shoulder, then froze.

Marc was standing behind her. He looked perfectly calm and in control but she noticed a little pulse that throbbed urgently at the edge of his jaw.

Wildly she looked at Chris but there was no escaping the inevitable.

Chris held out his hand. "Hello, Paul — long time, no see," he said easily as if there had been no animosity between them.

"How are you, Chris? Mrs Lynton?"

He looked enquiringly at Claire's mother but she made no attempt to shake hands with him, and only barely acknowledged his presence with a tight lipped expression and the briefest of nods.

Claire looked up, startled. There was now no escaping the fact that Marc knew who she was.

"Forgive me for intruding," Marc coolly seemed to have the situation under control. "I simply wished to say how much I enjoyed the concert and to offer my congratulations to Claire and," he turned and gave Jane a charming smile, "I'm sorry, I don't believe we've met."

"Jane, this is Paul Harris, or maybe you know him better as Marc Deloren," said Chris. "Paul, this is Jane, we are soon to be married, but no doubt Claire will have told you that."

"On the contrary," replied Marc, as he shook hands with Jane, "Claire speaks very little of her private life."

Claire felt the colour flood her

cheeks while Jane seemed to have been rendered speechless.

To ease the embarrassing silence that followed, Marc turned again to Chris. "So how's life treating you, these days?"

"Oh, mustn't grumble." Chris grinned good naturedly. "Don't need to ask you the same question."

Marc shrugged. "That's life, I suppose — each to his own."

"Chris has done very well for himself." At Mrs Lynton's abrupt interruption, everyone turned to look at her. Two bright spots of colour stained her cheeks and her eyes glittered behind her spectacles. "He's with the London Symphony Orchestra," she added sharply, then snapped her mouth shut into an uncompromising line.

Marc raised his eyebrows. "So you finally got your wish, Mrs Lynton. All that worrying was for nothing."

Mrs Lynton sniffed and looked away while the others looked from her to Marc in bewildered silence.

"I must ask you to excuse me," Marc looked at Claire as he spoke, then with a brief nod at the others, he turned and walked quickly away.

With a puzzled frown Claire looked from his retreating figure to Chris, then to her mother. "What did he mean?"

"I haven't the faintest idea," said Mrs Lynton briskly then in an obvious attempt to change the subject she leaned forward and lifted a plate of cakes. "Do have another cake Jane."

Chris however was not to be so easily put off. "Just a minute, Mum," he said, his eyes narrowing. "Paul said you'd finally got your wish. I don't understand. What wish was he talking about?"

Mrs Lynton shrugged and avoided her son's gaze but when it became obvious that he intended getting an answer, she said, "I only wanted what was best for you, Chris, you must understand that."

"Yes, Mum," Chris said patiently. "I

know all that, but I want to know what Paul meant."

Mary Lynton gazed round at the others then with an angry sigh, she said, "All I did was to make it perfectly plain to that young man that your future lay in classical music and not with the dreadful racket that he makes."

Carefully Chris set his cup down and stared incredulously at his mother. Slowly, choosing his words with great care, he said, "Are you saying you asked Paul to get rid of me?"

Claire found herself holding her breath as she waited for her mother's reply.

It seemed a long moment before Mrs Lynton finally found her voice. "Well, not in so many words . . . but like I said Christopher it was for your own good . . . "

"And all these years you let me think that he'd dropped me because I wasn't good enough?"

"But that's the whole point, you were too good for them. Just look how well you've done now — "

"They haven't done too badly either," Chris remarked grimly.

Claire glanced at him apprehensively. She'd rarely seen him so angry and certainly never with their mother.

As if trying to relieve the tension and avert a full-scale row, Jane suddenly stood up and looked at her watch. "We've a while before we need to go, so I'm going to chat to some of the others."

Claire too grabbed the opportunity to escape. "I need some fresh air," she muttered and pushing back her chair, she left Chris and her mother to sort out their differences. While Jane headed towards a group of their friends at another table, she pushed open the large glass doors and stepped thankfully out onto a balcony.

Leaning her arms on the stone parapet she gazed out across the beach to the sea beyond. She felt shocked by what she had just heard but while she felt sorry for her brother, at the same time she felt a tingle of something she found difficult to define when she thought of Marc and of how it seemed she might have misjudged him.

At that moment her attention was caught by a solitary figure who stood at the water's edge. With his hands thrust into his pockets he stood motionless, staring out to sea.

As she watched, something in the loneliness of his stance tugged at her heart and on a sudden impulse, she hurried along the balcony, down a flight of steps and onto the esplanade. It was relatively quiet at this time of day as most holidaymakers had returned to their hotels for dinner.

Lightly she ran across the road pausing only to slip off her high heeled shoes. Within moments she had reached his side and although he must have heard her approach across the shingle, he didn't turn. It was almost as if he had known she would come.

Quietly she stood beside him and looked out across the calm sea. Further along the beach two small boys were feeding a flock of sea-gulls that swooped around a breakwater but apart from them they were alone.

Bending down Marc picked up a flat pebble, balanced it in his hand then with a sideways flick of the wrist, sent it skimming across the waves.

After only a moment's hesitation Claire followed suit and between them they sent one pebble after another across the glass-like surface.

Then suddenly he caught Claire's wrist. She dropped the pebble she was about to throw and he whirled her round to face him.

"Claire." It was almost a groan, then he pulled her into his arms and his lips were against her hair, touching her eyelids, her cheeks and finally kissing away the salty tang on her own lips. Then as he drew away she was content to simply rest her head against his chest and listen to the steady beating of his heart until at last, she had to ask the question that was burning on her lips.

"When did you know who I was?"

He smiled and looked down at her and the intense blue of his eyes seemed to reflect the entire expanse of the sea.

"Not until Chillingham," he admitted. "It was Dave who told me."

"Ah," she breathed. "I thought Dave might have recognised me."

"It came to him suddenly in the middle of the concert. Apparently he'd puzzled over it ever since you joined us. He'd even asked me if I'd met you somewhere before. I said that I'd thought your face seemed familiar but he was insistent that he'd known you rather better than that. Mind you, Claire, you must admit you have changed a bit since schooldays."

She laughed and pulling away from him, stepped backwards as an adventurous wave threatened to lap over her feet. "I should hope I have." Then more seriously, she added, "Why did you come here today?"

"I was curious. I wanted to hear you play and after all, you were at my concert — "

"Were you terribly bored?"

"Bored? No. Why should I be? Were you bored at Chillingham?"

She laughed again. "Surprisingly, no. I've come to realise there are many ways of enjoying music."

"You play very well, Claire." The admiration was in his tone now as well as in his eyes. "You put your heart and soul into your performance."

"I could say the same about you."

He stared silently at her for a moment, then abruptly he said, "Have I wreaked havoc, back there?" He jerked his head towards the restaurant.

Claire shrugged. "I don't know. I left them to fight it out."

"Chris is a very talented musician. I understand he's doing very well."

"He was very upset when you dropped him. For ages he thought he wasn't any good." An accusatory note had crept into Claire's voice, then sharply she demanded, "But why did you drop him?"

Marc sighed and turned his head as if battling with some indecision, then he said, "It wasn't what you think, Claire. Chris is the finest rhythm guitarist I've ever heard. I'd have given my eye teeth to have had him with us when we turned professional."

"So why did you drop him? Surely it wasn't just because my mother told you she wanted him to be a classical musician?"

He glanced towards the restaurant. "She told you that?"

"Not in so many words, but she certainly implied it."

He hesitated again. "Well, it's partly true, but it was the way she went about it that decided me."

"Why, what did she do?" Claire stared at him suddenly fearful at what she might be about to hear.

"She did it through my mother."

"Your mother? But I didn't know she even knew your mother. Didn't you tell me that your mother had . . . " she trailed off embarrassed.

"That she'd died? Yes, she did and it was during the time that she was so ill that your mother came to see her. I remember coming home one day and Greta telling me that she'd had tea with your mother. Apparently she'd told her some story about how she'd promised Chris's father that she would do everything in her power to see that Chris studied the cello at music college. She pleaded with my mother to persuade me to 'let Chris go' as she put it but she didn't want Chris to know it was anything to do with her."

"But I still don't quite understand, if Chris was as good as you say, why did you go along with what she wanted?"

"For my mother. She was dying at the time."

"What?" Claire stared at him aghast.

"In all fairness, your mother didn't know that, but I would have done anything for my mother at that time so, against my better judgement, I did as she asked. I've always regretted it, until I learnt how well Chris had done, then I figured it had probably all been for the best."

"Except that it nearly destroyed his confidence," said Claire then added grimly, "But it was typical of my mother. Her ambition for us, Chris in particular, overshadowed everything and she is of course a snob, I know that; the pop business would have been unthinkable for her son."

Marc gave a rueful grin. "I suppose she thought she was doing the right thing."

"Oh, I don't doubt it. But it makes me furious to think of it; no wonder she looked startled when you appeared and why she was so worried when I went to work for you."

"Why didn't you say who you were?" he asked quietly when she fell silent.

She shrugged lightly. "I'd always disliked you for what I assumed you'd done to Chris and when you didn't recognise me, I thought it best to let things remain as they were."

"Was Chris badly upset when he was dropped?"

"Devastated."

Marc sighed angrily. "I'm beginning to understand your hostility now. I'd have acted the same in your shoes. But now you know the truth, does it make any difference?" Suddenly he sounded anxious and Claire smiled.

"It may do. Besides, I think I've become more tolerant since I've been with MDM."

"Don't tell me — you have even become crazy about my music."

She pulled a face. "I wouldn't quite go so far as to say that, although I'll admit I enjoyed Chillingham."

"It was magic, wasn't it?" His blue eyes sparkled and stepping forward, he took hold of her hands and staring down into her upturned face, he said, "Claire, have you thought about what I asked you?"

"About staying with the band?" Her

heart had begun to thud painfully at his nearness.

"Yes, and coming to the States with us?"

"My mother can't wait for me to leave MDM." She gave a rueful chuckle.

"It's not up to her. Let's face it, Claire, she does make a habit of interfering, doesn't she?"

"So how long do I have to make up my mind?"

He glanced at his watch. "Would ten minutes be enough?"

"I don't have ten minutes — I have to get back." She glanced over her shoulder at the restaurant as if she half expected to see her mother's disapproving figure at one of the windows.

He sighed. "Right, so you have to go, but don't take too long deciding."

They turned and in silence began to walk up the beach. It was Marc who finally spoke. "I have to go back to Whitcombe now." A note of tension had entered his voice and instinctively Claire knew that what had been troubling him at Chillingham was still worrying him. Then, he had wanted to talk. Had he now changed his mind?

Anxiously she glanced at him. "What is it?" she asked gently. "What's wrong, Marc? Can you tell me about it?"

He sighed. "I wish I could, Claire, but I can't. Not at the moment anyway . . . but soon maybe . . . " he trailed off, then on a brighter note, he said, "Why don't you come down to Whitcombe tomorrow and join me. We'll have a day off, I reckon we've earned one. We could go riding if you like."

Her heart leapt at the prospect. "What about Jasper? He'll be expecting me at MDM."

"You leave Jasper to me. Besides, we have business to discuss."

"Do we?" She raised her eyebrows and turned slightly as he followed her up the steps to the esplanade.

"Of course. You have your decision to give me."

She caught her breath then stiffened as she saw her family appear on the balcony. It was obvious that they were looking for her just as it was obvious from their expressions that they hadn't settled their differences.

"Oh dear," said Claire. "I really will have to go Marc. Chris will want to get started."

"Probably it will be best if I just disappear," said Marc quickly. "I'll send a car for you tomorrow at ten. O.K.?"

"You're the boss," Claire replied lightly but there was something about his smile as he turned, then hurried away, that seemed to melt her bones.

On the drive home Claire was almost thankful for the strained silence in the car. Chris and his mother quite obviously weren't speaking to each other and although Jane made one or two brave attempts at conversation, these were met by a stony silence but it gave Claire the opportunity to get her tangled thoughts into some sort of order.

She now knew without a shadow of doubt that instead of resisting Marc's attentions, she found herself longing for them. In spite of the fact that heartbreak would inevitably follow, she was powerless to control her overwhelming feelings for this man whom she'd previously so detested.

She also knew that she would be counting the hours until the following day when she would be meeting him at Whitcombe Manor.

7

CLAIRE slept only fitfully, so great on the one hand was her excitement at the prospect of spending the day with Marc but on the other, her fear that Serena would be at Whitcombe.

Serena was still as much of a mystery as ever. Claire was certain that no one at MDM knew of her existence for if they did there would have been gossip and the papers would have been full of speculation. But all had remained silent and Claire was forced to admit that she found it slightly unnerving.

Serena had seemed very much at home at Whitcombe Manor and that seemed to imply only one thing to Claire — that she was living with Marc. But if that were the case, why had Marc been showing her, Claire, so much attention? Why had he sung that song especially for her? Was it simply that he considered her a good assistant and didn't want her to leave MDM? But if that was the case, why had he kissed her? There had been passion in his kisses, that much she knew, but had he been merely stringing her along when all the time he was involved with the lovely dark haired beauty at his home?

For most of the night her tortured thoughts revolved in her head, mingling with dreams equally confusing so that when she awoke to the dawn chorus, she felt hollow-eyed but pent-up with tightly coiled tension as she contemplated the day ahead.

An early morning mist hung over the rooftops of Kingston but as Claire showered and dressed in jeans and a striped shirt, the sun broke through with all the promise of a warm sunny day.

Rummaging in the back of her wardrobe she found her leather riding-boots which had seen better days and a shabby tweed hacking jacket. She grimaced but thrust them into a carrier bag. She was ready far too early and spent the next hour fretting and fidgeting before Marc's chauffeur-driven car arrived to take her to Whitcombe Manor.

She hardly noticed the beauty of the surrounding countryside for today, as on her previous visit she felt far too nervous.

When they finally swept in through the gates she didn't know whether she was sorry or glad and as the car climbed the drive she wiped her damp palms on her jeans.

As the manor came into sight it was an immense relief to see Greta, her ample form swathed in a multi-coloured caftan, her hair escaping from its knot, standing on the lawns feeding two majestic-looking peacocks. She waved one plump hand as Claire stepped from the car then strolled across the velvety lawn to meet her.

"How beautiful they are." Claire

indicated the peacocks who had spread their magnificent tail feathers and were filling the air with their raucous cries.

"They are noisy creatures." Greta smiled and turned to enter the house. "But yes, you are right, so very beautiful. But they know it, my dear." She sighed. "Like the male of any species, I fear." then in the same breath she continued, "Marc is in the stables. Come through, I'll take you."

Claire fell into step beside the older woman giving her a curious glance as she did so. "Greta, why do you call him Marc? You must have known him when he was a child. I would have thought you would have been one of the few people to still call him Paul."

Greta didn't answer immediately, then as they crossed the oak panelled hall and took the passage to the kitchens, she lifted her plump shoulders in a shrug. "I like the name Marc, it suits him and now of course, it saves the confusion."

"Confusion? What do you mean?"

Claire frowned but Greta wasn't listening, for as they entered the kitchen they could see Marc leaning against the open doorframe. Casually dressed in dark cord trousers and a white open-necked shirt, he held a telephone in one hand while the receiver was tucked under his chin. Claire felt her breath catch in her throat.

As he caught sight of Greta and Claire he turned briefly away saying, "I'll get back to you later. Bye now."

Instinctively Claire knew he had been speaking to a woman and although there had been no sign of Serena, she eyed him warily as he replaced the telephone on one of the kitchen units then turned to face her.

"Hello." He smiled at her and Claire's heart lurched crazily. What was it about this man that had such a devastating effect on her — especially when she considered that until only very recently she'd all but detested him.

"I've been arranging a suitable horse

for you," he said. "How d'you fancy the strawberry roan you were admiring the last time you were here?"

She was surprised that he had remembered, but he mistook her expression.

"Perhaps you would prefer something more docile? There's Dolly, the grey, or even old Belinda, they don't come more docile than her."

"Oh no," replied Claire swiftly as she followed him into the sun dappled yard. "I enjoy a good ride." She pointed to the strawberry roan who had hopefully pushed her head over the stable door at the sound of their approach. "What's her name?"

"That's Gipsy, she's a real beauty." Mare opened the door of a tackroom next to the stall and after patting Gipsy's velvet nose Claire followed him. The tackroom was cool with flagstoned floor and whitewashed walls and an impressive display of leather saddles and bridles adorned three walls. A row of pegs on the remaining wall sported a selection of crops and riding-helmets.

"Help yourself, unless of course you have your own." Mare glanced at her carrier bag.

"No such luck, all I ever possessed was a tatty old hard hat, but I gather these helmets are the thing to wear these days," said Claire with a rueful grin. As Marc disappeared outside to help a groom to saddle up, she pulled on her boots and jacket and selected a helmet with emerald green, nylon colours.

Although she had told Marc she loved to ride, it had in fact, been a long time since she'd had the opportunity and as she stepped out into the yard again, she knew a moment's apprehension as she looked up at the strawberry roan who was standing waiting for her. Marc's stallion, Ebony, was having his girths tightened by the groom and as Claire hesitated, Marc moved round behind her.

"Let me give you a hand," he said

casually and as she gripped the reins and put one foot into the stirrup, he helped her to mount.

"Thanks," she smiled down at him, then watched as he lightly mounted Ebony. Slowly they circled the yard but Claire was only too aware of the horses' urgent need to be away.

Marc raised his hand to Greta who stood in the doorway watching them. Glancing up at the rows of latticed windows above the yard Claire wondered briefly if Serena could be up there also watching them or whether it had been her Marc had been speaking to on the telephone.

Then as the horses broke into a trot and they passed beneath a stone archway in a corner of the yard into the parkland beyond, she endeavoured to put all thoughts of Serena from her mind. It was her that Marc had asked to go with him, not Serena, or anyone else for that matter. She felt an almost forgotten thrill of excitement surge through her at the feel of the powerful animal beneath her, then she relaxed.

The mist of earlier had completely cleared and warm bright sunshine bathed the parkland before them. Majestic oaks dotted the emerald meadows and sheep grazed, lazily munching, only lifting their heads as the horses passed.

"How long is it since you've ridden?" Marc glanced sideways at her as he drew alongside.

"Too long," she replied, then added, "Why, does it show?"

"Not at all. You sit a horse beautifully. Where did you learn?"

"My father taught me. Horses were his passion."

"Is your father dead?"

Claire shook her head. "No, he and my mother split up ten years ago. He was her second husband and it never worked from the start. He trained horses for a living and after the divorce he emigrated to New Zealand."

"You miss him." It was a statement

rather than a question and she simply nodded in response. She always found it difficult to speak of her father with whom she'd always had more in common than with her mother.

They rode in silence, then leaving the parklands behind they climbed onto higher ground. As the track levelled out again, the horses broke into an easy canter and they rode together over short springy heather, between banks of yellow flowering gorse, its thickened woody stems twisted and bent in one direction by the wind.

Claire felt her cheeks tingle and the blood coursed through her veins as first Ebony, then Gipsy broke into a gallop.

Marc glanced once over his shoulder, then they both settled down to the pure thrill of the ride. They thundered for several miles across the short springy turf and it wasn't until they joined another bridle path that spiralled downwards into a valley, an emerald sea of curled bracken, that they slowed their pace. As they plunged into the cool, green darkness of a spinney, the horses' hooves a soft thud on the dusty leaf-mould, Marc reined in and turned in the saddle, waiting for her to join him.

As she rode up to him there was no mistaking the admiration on his face. "Your father was a good teacher. You're an excellent horsewoman."

She flushed at the praise. "I suppose you could say it's my second greatest love."

He raised his eyebrows. "Music being your first, of course."

"Of course." She smiled. "What amazes me is that we have now found two things we have in common."

"I think you may find there may be a few more than that."

She felt her pulses quicken at the look in his eyes before he dismounted and indicated for her to do the same.

As she slid from Gipsy's back, Claire found herself in Marc's arms as he helped her to the ground. For one brief moment as he continued to hold her, she closed her eyes and rested her head against the soft leather saddle. His grip tightened and suddenly she could deny it no longer. She loved him. The sudden flash of clarity made it all seem inevitable. In spite of everything; what he had been, what he had become and what he was now, whether or not they were compatible, whether he loved Serena — suddenly, none of it mattered. She only knew she loved him; loved him and wanted him more than she had ever wanted anything in her life.

With a little half-sigh she turned her head and looked at him and the look of tenderness she saw in his blue eyes, something she had never seen there before, gave her hope that he might be feeling the same way.

Gently he unfastened her helmet and as he removed it, he dropped a light kiss on her forehead, then disentangling the reins from her fingers, he led Gipsy and Ebony to a clump of saplings where he tethered them.

When he returned she saw he had discarded his own helmet. His dark hair was damp and ruffled. Without a word he took her hand leading her to a soft mossy hollow beneath the branches of a sycamore tree.

Claire sat down and Marc lowered his tall frame beside her, stretching out his long legs and linking his hands behind his head. With a deep sigh he gazed up through the branches of the sycamore to the vast blue expanse beyond then closing his eyes he lifted his face to the sunlight that filtered through the leaves.

Claire turned and looked at this man who in so many ways was as much a mystery now as he had always been. Carefully she studied the lean brown face, the straight nose, slightly flaring nostrils, the low brooding brows and the mass of tiny lines irradiating from his eyes. For years she had thought him conceited and arrogant, now, she knew that to be a front. Gradually she had come to realise there was so much more to him than she, or indeed any member of the public could have ever dreamed possible.

As if he sensed her scrutiny, he opened one eye then reaching out his hand he gripped her wrist and firmly drew her down beside him. Slipping his arm round her, he held her tightly against him, cradling her head in the hollow of his shoulder.

Perfectly contented, it was Claire's turn to close her eyes and relax.

Some time later when the only sound was the gentle humming of a bee and the far-away drone of a plane and when drowsiness was finally threatening to claim her, Claire became aware of a tremor through Marc's body. Opening her eyes she looked at him then realised with surprise that he was laughing.

"What is it?"

"I was just wondering what Jasper would say if he could see us now."

She smiled and snuggled more closely against him. "What did he say when you told him I wouldn't be in today?"

"He didn't comment. But I think he suspected we were spending the day together."

"I like Jasper," Claire said thoughtfully. "But I've just realised I know absolutely nothing about him — his private life, I mean. Is he married?"

"He was. He and his wife Rosa are divorced."

"Oh? Were there any children?"

"No." He grinned suddenly. "There was never any time for that," then growing serious he added, "Jasper is married to his work, haven't you noticed? That's why it never worked out with Rosa although he still visits her, in fact I would say they get on far better now than they ever did when they were married. It's like so many show-business marriages, they never stand a chance when one of the partners is away on tour for nine tenths of the year."

"Speaking of tours," Claire said quickly, wanting to divert the conversation away

184

from marriage, suddenly frightened by what she might hear. "You wanted to discuss the tour of the States."

"Have you decided yet?" She caught a sudden note of eagerness in his voice.

"Not entirely." She allowed a teasing note to creep into her tone. "But I'm working on it. After all, it isn't every day a girl gets the chance of a free trip to the States."

"That's true — and free it may be, but don't let anyone kid you it'll be easy. Believe me, it'll be the most gruelling month of your life."

"I don't doubt that — you're the worst slave-driver I've ever come across." She pouted slightly but secretly thought that she wouldn't care if she had to work twenty-four hours a day just so long as it meant being with him.

"You think you'll stand the pace?" he asked, and this time there was only concern in his manner and no trace of the mockery that there had been on the previous occasion he had asked the same question.

"Of course." She tilted her chin and he lifted one hand gently tracing a line down her cheek, then cupping her chin he gazed deeply into her eyes. "I don't doubt for one moment that you'll cope, not if Chillingham was anything to go by," he said softly. "But you know, Claire, it isn't only for your organising ability I want you on this trip."

"It isn't?" Her eyes widened at the same time as her heart leapt.

"No, I want to talk to you about some music arrangements with a view to using them on the tour."

Momentarily she felt a stab of disappointment because for one crazy moment she'd misunderstood and thought he'd wanted her for herself. Then slowly, she realised what he had said and she felt a new kind of excitement.

"What do you mean?" Eagerly she stared up at him, while he shifted slightly and sitting forward plucked a blade of grass, chewing it thoughtfully for a moment before answering her question.

At last, turning to her he asked, "Do you remember the awards ceremony and that arrangement of *Rogue Male* you played on Spike's keyboard?"

She nodded and felt the colour flood her cheeks. How could she ever forget.

Marc however seemed oblivious and continued eagerly. "I haven't been able to get that interpretation out of my head.

"I would never have thought of setting that number to a bolero beat — but it worked! It lifted the entire thing to another plane."

Claire was speechless, glowing at his words of praise. In the silence of the cool green of the spinney, Ebony suddenly whickered gently and she and Marc simultaneously looked to where the two horses quietly cropped the grass.

"When I watched you play at Brighton it gave me other ideas, exciting ideas," Marc went on and now there was an air of such enthusiasm about him that Claire noticed the worried, tense look which seemed to have haunted him for days had all but disappeared.

"What I would like to do is to combine our music, yours and mine. That symphony you played — Brahms, wasn't it? Well, I can just hear one of our numbers, *Night Rhythm*, played against that sort of arrangement with a string accompaniment. What do you think, Claire?" Eagerly he searched her face. "Are you willing to give it a try? We could make a start when we get back to the manor, we have the piano there."

So she would actually get to play that wonderful instrument in the drawing-room of Whitcombe Manor. So why did she still feel disappointed?

As she wrestled with conflicting emotions — the heady elation that he should want her to help with his music and the growing awareness of her love for him, together with the dread that that love would never be reciprocated, he suddenly said, "You know, Claire there's another reason I wanted you with us."

"There is?" she whispered, holding her breath.

"It isn't only your music," his voice suddenly grew husky. "It's you, I can't get you out of my mind. You're there all the time." Gently he took her face between his hands and as his lips claimed hers in a kiss of such passion and tenderness, she stopped trying to reason things out and simply gave herself up to the ecstasy of the moment.

Later as they lay staring up through the mantle of leaves above them, Marc stirred and taking Claire's hand, he one by one gently uncurled her fingers.

"Claire, you've guessed that I have problems at the moment." She nodded and he continued, "As I said before, I'm not able to discuss them, even with you. All I ask is that you trust me and

189

give me time." As he spoke, he glanced at his watch, "Speaking of time, I'm afraid I have to get back now as I'm expecting a phone call."

With a little sigh of reluctance, she stood up. With the mention of a phone call the spell had been broken. No doubt it would be from Serena but as she fastened her helmet while Marc untethered the horses, she gave herself a little shake. Hadn't he just asked her to trust him?

They left the spinney and climbed the path through the bracken, then once on level ground again they broke into an easy canter but it seemed to Claire that their secret had been left behind in that cool green hollow.

When they were about a mile from the manor, Marc who was ahead of Claire, suddenly reined in, Ebony rearing at the interruption to his stride. Marc lifted his head and appeared to be listening then as Claire reached him she too heard the drone of an aircraft.

Looking back over her shoulder she

saw a familiar red and white helicopter flying low and as it passed over them, Gipsy too reared then kicked her back legs.

Claire was so intent on bringing the horse under control that when she looked up again, she was surprised to see that Marc had set Ebony at a gallop in the direction of the manor.

She followed at a rather more leisurely pace but at the same time wondering why the sight of his helicopter should have brought such a dramatic response from Marc.

When she entered the parklands surrounding Whitcombe Manor the first thing she saw was that the helicopter had landed outside the stable walls. As she drew nearer she could see that the pilot was still seated at the controls and the rotor blades were whirring. There was no sign of Marc.

She turned Gipsy towards the stables then passed beneath the stone archway, the horse's hooves echoing on the cobbles. In the yard a groom was leading Ebony into his stall while Marc, struggling into a leather jacket, was hurrying towards the archway. But it was the figure by his side who caused Claire's heart to lurch sickeningly. Serena, her blue black hair flowing over her shoulders and dressed in a simple cream dress was clutching Marc's arm and almost running to keep up with him.

As Claire reached them Serena didn't even seem to see her but Marc paused briefly while Serena hurried on towards the waiting helicopter. Reaching up he briefly took hold of Claire's arm.

"Claire, I'm sorry. I have to go. I'll explain everything later."

She stared down at him noting the distracted look on his face. Then he was gone, running to join Serena. Claire swivelled in the saddle and with a pang she saw him join her and the pilot in the cockpit, then the door closed and immediately the machine took off, rising rapidly, banking to the left, then disappearing behind a clump of pine trees.

With a sick feeling deep inside, Claire urged Gipsy on into the centre of the yard and dismounted. The groom came out of Ebony's stall and she handed him Gipsy's reins. With a last pat of thanks on the horse's velvet nose, Claire watched as the groom led her away.

Disconsolately she turned towards the house. What should she do now? Obviously going with Serena meant far more to Marc than spending the rest of the day with her, so she might as well get used to the fact, she thought with a sudden surge of anger as she walked towards the kitchen door. Then as she recalled the look on his face when he had stared up at her, she softened slightly. Maybe it had been something very important and he had said he would explain everything later.

She tapped lightly on the door and pushed it open. The kitchen however was deserted and idly she wondered where Greta was. Thinking she heard a sound in the hall, she stepped out of the kitchen but on going to investigate, she found that too was empty. The drawing-room door was open and she looked inside the big room. The grand piano stood in the window and with a rueful look, she thought that it seemed as if she were fated never to play it. She couldn't quite bring herself to break the silence in the house even though she felt sure that Marc wouldn't mind if she did play without him being there.

Even as she debated what she should do next, she heard voices outside on the lawn. Crossing to the window she placed her hands on the oak sill and looked out.

The peacocks were once again strutting and parading on the lawns and as before Greta was feeding them. Claire smiled, then she realised that this time Greta was not alone. A small boy, no more than five or six years old was jumping excitedly up and down as the peacocks fanned their tails.

As Claire watched, Greta held out her hand to the child who turned and ran excitedly across the lawn towards the house. The pair disappeared from her view and seconds later Claire heard the front door open followed by the high-pitched chatter of the child. She wondered who he was for she'd never heard any mention of a child at Whitcombe before.

Slowly she walked out of the drawing-room into the hall. Greta turned and catching sight of Claire, she smiled, "You enjoy your ride, yes?"

"Very much, thank you, it was lovely to . . . " Claire trailed off as the child, who had been picking up a handful of peacock feathers which he had dropped on the black-and-white tiled floor, suddenly looked up at her. He was such a beautiful child there was no denying that, with his mop of dark curls and olive colouring.

"Hello," he said unblinkingly. "What's your name?"

"Hello," she replied weakly, hearing

her voice as if it came from a great distance while in her mind a dreadful possibility was beginning to take shape. "My name's Claire."

"Mine's Paul. I haven't seen you before."

Greta had begun to climb the great staircase but she paused, one plump hand on the bannister. "Come along now," she said to the child. "Time to wash before lunch."

"I want to talk to Claire," said the child, gathering up his feathers. "Then I want to see Daddy."

"Later, come on," replied Greta. Claire stood as if transfixed, then as the child began to climb the stairs, she stepped forward. "Greta?"

"Yes?"

"What did he say his name was?" She swallowed. Suddenly she had to know. Whatever the truth might be, she had to know.

By this time the child had scampered on up the stairs ahead of Greta and as he reached the top, he kneeled down and peered at them through the bannisters.

"That's Paul," replied Greta and there was no mistaking the affection in her voice.

"Who . . . who is Paul exactly?" said Claire holding her breath, as Greta, who by this time was halfway up the stairs, turned and looked back at her.

"You don't know? No, of course you don't. How could you? He's Serena's son."

8

AFTER the initial shock a gradual numbness crept up on Claire and she knew that if she didn't do something soon, she would be rendered incapable. Refusing to allow herself to even think about what she had discovered, she walked through the front door and round the west side of the manor to the garages.

She eventually found Williams, the chauffeur, in an old coach house drinking tea and playing cards with the groom and one of the gardeners. All three jumped guiltily when Claire appeared in the open doorway.

"I'm sorry to trouble you," she faltered, then looking at Williams she said, "Could you drive me home, please?"

Williams noisily pushed his chair back and struggled to his feet surprise showing on his face. "Why, of course, Miss. But I understood you would be staying all day and that Mr Deloren would be taking you home himself."

So that was what he had planned, Claire thought bitterly. Trying to keep her face expressionless, she said, "Mr Deloren has been called away and I need to return home."

"Very well, Miss." Williams drained his cup and picking up his peaked cap from the table, he grimaced at the others then followed Claire outside.

There was no further sign of Greta or the child and it was with a sense of relief that Claire slid into the rear seat of the Daimler. As the car drew away she kept her eyes straight, not once looking back at Whitcombe Manor.

During the drive to Kingston, Claire still didn't allow her thoughts to focus on what had happened although she was only too aware of Williams' puzzled expression when he glanced at her in his driving mirror.

At last in the sanctuary of her flat

she finally gave way to her emotions in a torrent of weeping.

How could Marc have done this to her? How could he have led her on, led her to believe that his problems could easily be resolved when all along he and Serena had a son!

She didn't know whether they were married or not but even if they weren't, it was perfectly obvious that they had shared the closest of relationships for a very long time. The child who even bore his real name, Paul, was at least five years old. But what Claire found almost impossible to accept was how they had managed to keep the whole affair a secret.

She recovered sufficiently to make herself a badly needed cup of tea and as she curled herself into the corner of her old sofa, she found herself thinking how incredible it was that the press hadn't got hold of the story or, if not the press, then his fans. Then on reflection she supposed that it was his fans and his image that was probably the purpose of the secrecy.

A married star in his position just didn't possess the same charisma as one who was free. But if that were so, what of his supposed affairs with other women? Had they merely been a front or was he in the habit of infidelity?

Feeling the tears flood her eyes again she set down her cup and saucer on a coffee table beside the sofa and taking out her handkerchief she blew her nose hard. How could she have let herself be so taken in by him? Why, she was no better than the groupies who followed the tours. Why, oh why, hadn't she trusted her first instincts and kept him at arm's length? Why had she allowed herself to fall in love? If she hadn't, she wouldn't now be suffering this physical pain.

By the time Claire had finished her tea one thing had become perfectly clear; not only could she no longer contemplate accompanying the band on their tour of the States but she could no longer even remain employed by MDM.

Her letter of resignation she addressed to Jasper finding it impossible to even write Marc's name and after all, it had been Jasper who had employed her.

She made several attempts at the letter all of them ending in tiny pieces in her waste bin until at last, she managed a note that was both brief and to the point. She told Jasper that owing to personal reasons which she found difficult to discuss, it was impossible for her to remain in the employment of MDM. She went on to apologise for any inconvenience she might cause as her absence would be immediate.

Her hands shook as she sealed the envelope and glancing at her watch she realised that if she hurried, she would catch the late afternoon post.

The regret she felt as she dropped the letter into the postbox at the corner of the road almost overwhelmed her for quite apart from the intensity of her feelings for Marc, she knew she would miss her job. This seemed incredible now to Claire when she recalled how much she had disliked the set-up when she had first joined MDM and of how she couldn't wait to leave. Without her being aware of it, it had become her whole life; the excitement of the action-packed days, the challenge of organising the seemingly impossible and the friendship of the others. Jasper, she knew, she would miss desperately for she had become very fond of the zany little character.

Slowly, with dragging steps, she climbed the stairs to her flat and as she fitted the key in the lock she heard her phone ringing. Her first thought was that it might be Marc but by the time she'd opened the door the ringing had stopped. She stared at the silent phone. Had it been Marc? But why should it be? He was most probably living it up somewhere with Serena — he wouldn't have the time to spare her a second thought.

Her heart twisted painfully and she turned and walked slowly into her bedroom. Her riding-boots were on the rug where she had dumped them. The mere sight of them reminded her of how perfect the day had been until the fateful arrival of the helicopter. She still wasn't certain whether Serena had come in the helicopter or whether she had been at Whitcombe Manor all the time, but either way, it made no difference. It was as if the early part of the day hadn't happened, as if it had all been a dream.

Idly she wandered from her bedroom into her tiny kitchen where she half-heartedly attempted to prepare herself something to eat. She realised she hadn't eaten all day. Normally she would have been starving, now, the sight of food made her feel nauseous. She struggled with each mouthful of a cheese sandwich then jumped when the phone suddenly rang again.

Cautiously she lifted the receiver. "Hello?"

"Hello, Claire?"

Her heart sank as she heard her mother's voice. "Yes, hello, Mum. How are you?"

"I'm well. But Claire there's something I want to say to you. Something that's been worrying me since yesterday."

There was something curiously subdued about her mother's usually sharp tone and Claire waited for her to continue.

"First of all, Claire, I owe you an apology."

"What for?"

"The way I behaved over Paul Harris," her mother replied, coming straight to the point.

"Oh," replied Claire then fell silent as she battled with strong emotions evoked simply by the sound of his name.

"You see, Claire, over that business with Chris, well, I did what I felt to be the right thing at the time. Can you understand that?"

"Yes, Mum . . . I suppose so . . . "

"I only ever had your best interests at heart, yours and Chris's, you know. It wasn't easy after Chris's father died and then later, what with your father going . . . and everything."

"No, of course not." Claire had never heard her mother talk in this fashion before and she felt at a loss to know what to say. The way she was feeling didn't help and she found she had to concentrate hard on what her mother was trying to explain.

"I had a long talk with Chris last night. Jane went to see her parents which was a good thing, because Chris and I needed to clear the air. He told me a lot of things about Paul Harris that I didn't know."

"He did?" Claire said faintly.

"Yes, and I'm ready to admit that I might have been wrong in my opinion of that young man. For a start, I didn't realise the amount of work he did for charity — "

"I did try to tell you — "

"I know you did, but I wasn't

prepared to listen. Well, I was wrong. And there's another thing, apparently he's given a home all these years to a rather peculiar refugee woman whom his mother befriended. I must say, with all things considered, it does seem I've misjudged him. Anyway, what I was coming to, Claire, was that Chris and I rather thought that you seemed keen on carrying on with that job of yours and I didn't want you to be influenced by anything I might have said."

"No, Mum." Claire sighed. "I won't be."

"Oh." Her mother paused fractionally, then said, "Chris did say also that Jane felt that there could be more to it — between you and Paul Harris, I mean. Is that so, Claire?"

Claire took a deep breath. "No, Mum. Jane was wrong."

"Oh, we rather thought . . . well . . . we thought what with him coming down to hear you play at Brighton and you mentioning to Jane about a trip to America . . . "

"I won't be going to America."

"Oh."

"In fact, Mum, you may as well know now. I won't be working for MDM anymore."

A silence greeted her announcement while Claire was forced to bite her lip to hold back her tears.

"Claire, I do hope it wasn't anything to do with that scene at the hotel yesterday. Was it anything I said?"

Claire swallowed knowing that she couldn't continue talking for very much longer. "Look, Mum, I'm sorry but I don't want to talk about it at the moment. I'll ring you back later."

Without giving her mother a chance to say another word, Claire hung up, choking back her tears as she did so. For a brief moment she rested her forehead against the wall. How ironic that while she thought there had been a chance of a relationship with Marc, her mother had detested him and everything he stood for, and now that it was impossible, her mother was almost falling over backwards to say what a nice fellow he really was.

If she hadn't been feeling so wretched Claire would most certainly have seen the funny side of the situation. As it was, she turned miserably away and when the phone rang again almost immediately, she chose to ignore it. She just couldn't cope with anymore from her mother.

Claire spent a fitful night haunted by wild dreams where Jasper and the band's drummer, Zac, were chasing her on a pair of black stallions while a helicopter hovered dangerously overhead. The whirring rotor blades came closer and closer to her and as she opened her mouth to scream, she suddenly awoke.

With her heart pounding she lay in a cold sweat, then as memory flooded back, she groaned and buried her face in the pillow.

She had nothing to get up for that morning, no job to go to, but in spite of her lethargy, she found it impossible to go back to sleep. She knew she should probably get herself down to the job centre but for a long time she lacked the inclination to even get out of bed.

At last she roused herself and after a shower she had to admit she felt a little better. She dressed in jeans and a sweat-shirt then went downstairs to collect her post and the morning paper.

The only letter did little to raise her spirits for it was a bill from British Telecom which she thrust into her pocket, then picking up the newspaper and scanning the headlines she went slowly back upstairs.

Once back in her flat she filled the kettle and while waiting for it to boil, she unfolded the paper and spread it over the kitchen table turning to the gossip page. Her gaze immediately came to rest on a large photograph that dominated the page and as she recognised the two people in the picture she froze.

Quickly she scanned the caption which read, "Rumour has been rife lately that there is a new, mystery woman in the life of Rock Star Marc Deloren. Speculation was heightened recently at his Charity Concert at Chillingham Hall when he dedicated one of his songs, *Stay With Me*, to an anonymous woman in the audience. He has never been known to do this before and since then, the media and his fans have been kept guessing as to the identity of the woman. Yesterday, however, in London our photographer caught him with this stunningly beautiful lady. He declined to give her name thereby confirming her as the Mystery Woman. The couple were pictured outside the . . . "

With a sick feeling in the pit of her stomach, Claire screwed up the paper, unable to read any further and as she pushed the paper into her waste bin the doorbell rang.

Desperately struggling to compose herself she opened the door.

Jasper stood on the landing.

Claire stared at him in amazement. He looked even wilder and more frantic than usual in his striped suit and shocking pink shirt. "Jasper! Whatever are you doing here?"

"You may well ask. Someone's got to sort things out and as usual, it's me. Tell me, Claire, what the hell is going on?"

"I don't know what you mean," Claire eyed him suspiciously.

"Did you get my letter?"

"Of course. I tore it up."

"I meant it, Jasper. Every word of it."

"Well if that's the case, why has your mother been on the phone demanding to know why we've sacked you?"

"What!" She stared at him in horror.

"That's right. Now, are you going to ask me in?"

Absent-mindedly she stood aside for him to enter the flat. She was still reeling from the fact that her mother had been interfering again.

As she shut the door and followed Jasper into the lounge, he turned and spread his hands. "I didn't even have time for a quiet nervous breakdown when I read your letter, before I was told that your mother was on the phone."

"But what did she say exactly?"

"Simply that she thought you'd been given the sack by Marc because she had somehow offended him when she'd met him at Brighton on Sunday. I didn't have a clue what she was going on about. In fact, I didn't even know Marc had been to Brighton. I tell you, no one ever thinks to inform me about anything! Anyway, before I have time to even think, Marc's on the blower."

"And what did he have to say?" Claire's tone was suddenly cold and Jasper looked sharply at her.

"He seemed to have more of an idea what was going on than I did. He was upset about your resignation though. He said he'd been trying to ring you but that you weren't answering your phone. He wants me to take you to meet him." He glanced at his watch. "Can we go now, love? I'm running late as it is."

"I'd rather not, Jasper. I'm sorry but there really isn't anymore to say. I can't . . . I can't work for Marc anymore . . . " Her voice faltered and Jasper suddenly narrowed his eyes and peered at her keenly.

"Hey, what is it? What's wrong? Tell old Jasper all about it."

She shook her head, not trusting her voice any further.

"Listen, love, if this is about what I suspect, then all I can say is, I think you should come with me now and give Marc a chance to explain."

"What's the point?"

"I'm the point. Me! D'you understand? I hope you can sort out your differences with Marc, but if you don't, then I'm not going to lose the best assistant I've ever had or I'm ever likely to have. O.K.? Right, so no more arguing, get your coat and come with me."

Ten minutes later Claire found herself seated beside Jasper in his Volvo as he impatiently negotiated the morning traffic. She remained silent until they roared past the MDM building then she turned to him in surprise.

"Where are we going?"

"Knightsbridge." His reply was non-committal.

"Knightsbridge?" she echoed. "Whatever for?"

"Orders." He shrugged, taking his hands precariously from the wheel. "Ours is not to reason why."

"But I don't understand. Who's in Knightsbridge?"

"Presumably, Marc. But don't ask me why, honey, I'd be the last to know anyone's reasons for doing anything around here. He just gave me an address in Knightsbridge, asked me to pick you up and take you there."

"It wouldn't be his London home by any chance?" Suddenly she was alarmed. If it were, there was a very good chance that Serena would be there and that, she didn't feel she could handle.

Jasper shook his head. "No, that's in Kensington. It's no good, honey, your guess is as good as mine — you'll just have to wait and see."

Claire was silent for the remainder of the journey, hardly daring to wonder what Marc wanted.

When Jasper finally drew onto the forecourt of a large elegant building and they stepped from the car, she was amazed to read the brass plaque beside the entrance which stated that the building was a private hospital.

Puzzled she turned to Jasper but it was quite obvious that he was equally surprised.

A smartly dressed woman answered the door and when Jasper announced who they were, she smiled. "Do come in. Mr Harris is waiting for you."

Jasper raised his eyebrows then they followed the woman down a richly carpeted corridor. Claire shook her head in response to Jasper's unformed question. She too had no idea why Marc should be using his real name, or for that matter, what he was doing in this obviously exclusive clinic.

The woman paused before a door, knocked, then turned the handle. She opened the door, then with a smile stepped aside for Jasper and Claire to enter the room.

Claire saw Marc immediately, he was sitting on the arm of a red velvet sofa. Serena was by his side and he had one arm protectively around her shoulders.

At the sight of them, Claire's heart twisted painfully. Why had she come? What was she doing here? How dare Marc send for her! Had he done so simply to rub salt into her wounds?

Marc stood up and in spite of her anguish, Claire noticed how tired he looked, almost as if he hadn't slept that night. A quick glance at Serena however showed her to be absolutely radiant. If she had seemed beautiful before it was nothing compared to now.

With shining eyes she was gazing up at Marc.

"Jasper," said Marc, "you've brought Claire. Thanks." As he spoke he looked past Jasper to Claire, giving her his heart stopping smile.

"Well, Marc, I don't know what's going on," said Jasper with an exaggerated sigh. "And I haven't the time to stop and find out." He glanced at his watch. "I've to be at Broadcasting House at midday; there's a contract to negotiate — some of us have to work, you know." His remark was pointed but it was lost on Marc who merely grinned as Jasper turned to leave.

As he passed Claire, the little manager touched her shoulder. She found the gesture both comforting and endearing and taking a deep breath she walked right into the room.

"You wanted to see me," she said quietly, looking directly at Marc.

"Yes, Claire," he replied. "I'm not able to leave here at the moment and we have things to discuss."

"We have?" She raised her eyebrows but before Marc had time to enlarge, the door opened again and the woman who had showed them in, came into the room.

Looking at Serena, she said, "You may go in now."

The look that Serena gave Marc caused Claire to stiffen and a shaft of pain seemed to slice into her body.

Serena jumped to her feet and Claire noticed she was wearing the same cream dress she had been wearing the previous afternoon, but now it was crumpled and her thick lustrous hair was tousled and uncombed. Claire also noticed as Serena walked towards her that she too looked very tired in spite of her obvious happiness.

As she reached Claire, she smiled shyly at her, then she turned to Marc. "Are you coming with me?" Her large dark eyes were suddenly anxious.

He shook his head, then took hold of her hand and holding it tightly, he lifted it briefly to his lips. "No, you go in first. I'll be along later." He watched her walk out of the room.

"Why did you ask Jasper to bring me here?" Claire suddenly blurted out and there was a note of anguish in her tone which he couldn't fail to notice.

He narrowed his eyes. "I asked him to bring you because I've heard two very strange rumours this morning. One was that I was supposed to have sacked you from MDM and the other was that you had resigned anyway. I don't understand either."

"They are easily explained. My mother rang me last night and I told her that I wouldn't be working for you anymore. She must have got hold of the wrong end of the stick and thought that you had sacked me."

"Why would she think that?"

"She was concerned about her attitude towards you at Brighton, she thought you might have been influenced by it."

"It sounds as if she may have changed her tune where I'm concerned. The last

I heard she couldn't wait for you to leave."

"That's true, but apparently she had a long talk with Chris; he must have put in a good word for you."

"Good old Chris — I owe him one — but that still doesn't answer my other question."

"Your other question?" Claire tried to sound casual but she knew her cheeks had started to burn and she was only too aware of his nearness.

"Come on, Claire, you know what I mean. Why your resignation?"

Suddenly she was unable to meet the expression in his brilliantly blue eyes and sick at heart, she turned away. "I should have thought that was obvious." Her voice was husky.

"The only reason I can think of is that you're angry with me for abandoning you yesterday. If that's it, then I apologise but I'd like the chance to explain . . . "

"It wasn't only that . . . "

"Then what?" Stepping nearer, he

stretched out his hand and gently lifted her chin, tilting her face towards him.

"You haven't been honest with me."

"I don't understand."

"Oh, Marc please! No more games. For some time now you've led me to believe there could be more to our relationship . . . why, only yesterday in the spinney . . . I thought . . . I . . . "

"Yes, Claire?" he murmured softly, so close now that she could feel his warm breath on her cheek. "What did you think?"

"I thought . . . I thought — Oh, what the hell does it matter what I thought. It can't make any difference."

"Why can't it?"

"Well, for a start, there's Serena!"

He frowned. "Serena? What's she got to do with anything?"

Claire stared at him incredulously. "I would have thought she has everything to do with it."

"I don't see why . . . "

"And why all the secrecy?" she demanded, not allowing him to continue.

"I suppose that was in case the press or your fans got wind of it?"

"That's true. But how did you know . . . ?"

"It would ruin your image wouldn't it?" Relentlessly she went on.

"My image?" He looked bewildered. "Claire, what are you talking about?"

"It's a fact, isn't it, that rock stars' popularity wanes once they are married and probably even more so once they have children?" Her voice broke and she pulled away from him.

"Claire, I wish you'd explain what you mean. I haven't a clue what you're talking about."

"I saw the child, Paul, yesterday after you'd made your dramatic exit," she flung at him.

"Did you?" His bewilderment temporarily lifted and his blue eyes lit up. "What did you think of him? He's a great little guy isn't he? But what did you mean about my image and having children? Hey, Claire," sudden realisation flared in his eyes, "you didn't think Paul was my son?"

It was her turn to look bewildered. "Yes, I did."

"Oh, Claire . . . "

"So whose son is he?"

"Serena's."

"Well, I gathered that much!" She was unable to keep the sarcasm from her voice.

He stared at her, then suddenly narrowing his eyes, he said, "Claire, Serena isn't my wife — you didn't think that, did you?"

She lowered her eyes, unable to face his questioning gaze.

For a long moment Marc continued to stare at her, then he gave a deep sigh and taking her by the shoulders he said, "Claire, look at me. Please, look at me and listen."

Slowly she raised her eyes to his and the tenderness in their depths caused her heart to pound.

"Serena is my best friend's wife."

"What!"

"Yes. She's married to Stephan Cole.

Paul is their son."

"Stephan Cole?" Claire frowned, she'd heard that name somewhere before.

"Yes, Stephan and I went through school together, he was one of the original members of the band."

Claire stared at him as something that Chris had said clicked into place. "But didn't you sack him from the band?"

"Sack him? Good God no. Wherever did you get that idea? Stephan is a fantastic composer. He wrote most of our original material. The band is indebted to him, in fact you could say he was responsible for our early success."

"Then why? . . . I don't understand . . . "

"Stephan's great ambition was to go solo. He left the band of his own free will and went to the States where he met Serena. Then everything started to go wrong for him. He didn't get the contracts he needed, his health suffered

225

and he rapidly went downhill. I tried to keep in touch with him but he's very proud and I didn't hear from him for some years. Then one day, right out of the blue, I received a letter from Serena asking for my help. Stephan was seriously ill and needed urgent treatment that they couldn't pay for."

"But why didn't you tell me? What has all the secrecy been about?" Even as she demanded his explanation a tiny germ of hope was stirring deep inside her.

Gently he led her to the sofa and drew her down beside him enfolding her in his arms as he did so.

"Stephan is suffering from a kidney complaint, he was on constant dialysis and needed a transplant. I arranged for the three of them to come here and for Stephan to be admitted to this hospital to await a donor."

"Did no one know?"

"Only Greta, who knew Stephan when he was a boy. Besides, I wanted Serena and Paul to stay at Whitcombe

Manor with Greta."

"I still don't understand the need for secrecy."

He sighed. "On reflection, I suppose I should have told Jasper, and you of course." He tightened his grip as he spoke and she moved even closer against him. "But I felt it wouldn't have been fair. It's been a very traumatic time and Stephan's been at death's door on more than one occasion. I didn't want the press to get hold of the story, they would have loved it and they would have hounded you and Jasper if they got wind of it. You can just imagine it. The drama of the wait for a suitable donor. There's no way I want that sort of publicity. My friends are very special to me and I wanted total privacy for them, not the sort of circus that would have followed if the press had found out." Anxiously he turned to her. "You do understand, don't you?"

She nodded slowly and bit her lip.

How wrong they had all been about this man.

"Oh, Claire, my poor little love. What I must have put you through. To think you thought that Serena and I were married!"

"Well, I didn't think that at first, I just thought maybe you were having a relationship, then I saw Paul and Greta told me that he was Serena's son and well, I suppose I just put two and two together . . . "

"And came up with five." He laughed and turning her face towards him, he covered her lips with his own in a kiss which kindled such passion in Claire that it removed any traces of doubt in her mind.

A long time later he drew away but she remained with her head cradled against his shoulder. "Marc?" she said at last breaking the silence.

"Umm?" He sounded contented, lazy even.

"What did happen yesterday?"

"You mean the helicopter and all

that drama? They found a donor for Stephan. Some poor guy in a road smash on the M6. He was carrying a donor card and his tissue was found to be compatible with Stephan's."

She sat up straight and stared at Marc. "You mean . . . ?"

"That's right." He gave her no time to continue. "They operated in the night. So far Stephan is doing well. Apparently the next twenty-four hours will be critical but the surgeon came to see us just before you arrived and he said we had every reason to be optimistic."

"Oh, Marc. I'm so pleased. That explains why Serena looked so radiant."

"Yes, that's about the right word for it. She worships Stephan, you know. And he's pretty special to me too. The last few weeks haven't been exactly easy."

"I realise that now. Both Jasper and I were aware that you had problems, that you were under great stress."

"Did Jasper have any theories what

it might all be about?" He grinned suddenly.

"He just said it must be your love life."

"Which didn't help you much. Well, my love, it's all over now."

"I suppose I'd better put Jasper out of his misery and tell him that I won't be resigning after all."

"Well . . . that's debatable . . . "

"What do you mean?"

"He may just have to find a new assistant after all."

"Why?" She struggled upright and turned to look at him.

"Like I said to you yesterday, I shall be needing your help with musical arrangements, you have your own career to pursue and any spare time you have, I hope you'll concentrate on just being my wife."

"Whatever will your fans think about that?"

"Never mind my fans, what about your mother?"

Claire laughed and just before his

lips again claimed hers she said, "Well, my mother did say she only wanted what was best for me and there can't be any doubt about what that is."

THE END

WITH SOMEBODY ELSE
Theresa Charles

Rosamond sets off for Cornwall with Hugo to meet his family, blissfully unaware of the shocks in store for her.

A SUMMER FOR STRANGERS
Claire Hamilton

Because she had lost her job, her flat and she had no money, Tabitha agreed to pose as Adam's future wife although she believed the scheme to be deceitful and cruel.

VILLA OF SINGING WATER
Angela Petron

The disquieting incidents that occurred at the Vatican and the Colosseum did not trouble Jan at first, but then they became increasingly unpleasant and alarming.

DOCTOR NAPIER'S NURSE
Pauline Ash

When cousins Midge and Derry are entered as probationer nurses on the same day but at different hospitals they agree to exchange identities.

A GIRL LIKE JULIE
Louise Ellis

Caroline absolutely adored Hugh Barrington, but then Julie Crane came into their lives. Julie was the kind of girl who attracts men without even trying.

COUNTRY DOCTOR
Paula Lindsay

When Evan Richmond bought a practice in a remote country village he did not realise that a casual encounter would lead to the loss of his heart.